"Should ⸻ the Ki⸻ ⸻"

His tone was amused yet sympathetic at the same time.

"I don't think that will be necessary," Gabi answered with a forced air of indifference that failed to hide her momentary discomposure.

"The kiss of peace, then, in hopes of calling a cease-fire in this war of wills that exists between us." Peter didn't give Gabi time to think of a rejoinder; he was already easing her down onto the ground.

Gabi opened her mouth to protest and was met with a kiss that pressed her head against the earth. She tried to wriggle out of Peter's embrace but was held fast by the weight of his chest and by his elbows, which prevented any sideways movement of her body. Her immobility left her angry and frustrated; and then her resentment was washed away in the flood of sweet desire that was unleashed by his deep, penetrating kiss.

CHERYL DURANT

has traveled in twenty different countries around the world. Captivated by the literary life, she has worked as an editor, literary agent and copywriter at various times, as well as being an author.

Dear Reader:

SILHOUETTE DESIRE is an exciting new line of contemporary romances from Silhouette Books. During the past year, many Silhouette readers have written in telling us what other types of stories they'd like to read from Silhouette, and we've kept these comments and suggestions in mind in developing SILHOUETTE DESIRE.

DESIREs feature all of the elements you like to see in a romance, plus a more sensual, provocative story. So if you want to experience all the excitement, passion and joy of falling in love, then SILHOUETTE DESIRE is for you.

I hope you enjoy this book and all the wonderful stories to come from SILHOUETTE DESIRE. I'd appreciate any thoughts you'd like to share with us on new SILHOUETTE DESIRE, and I invite you to write to us at the address below:

Karen Solem
Editor-in-Chief
Silhouette Books
P.O. Box 769
New York, N.Y. 10019

CHERYL DURANT
Bittersweet In Bern

Silhouette Desire

Published by Silhouette Books New York

America's Publisher of Contemporary Romance

SILHOUETTE BOOKS, a Simon & Schuster Division of
GULF & WESTERN CORPORATION
1230 Avenue of the Americas, New York, N.Y. 10020

Distributed by Pocket Books

ISBN: 0-671-42760-1

First Silhouette Books printing October, 1982

10 9 8 7 6 5 4 3 2 1

America's Publisher of Contemporary Romance

Printed in the U.S.A.

1

Gabi Studer was bored. When she had accepted a job as secretary in the Chicago advertising agency of Yates, Frank, & Bingham, she had been led to believe that it would be an exciting position full of opportunities for personal growth. "You'll work for the creative director," the assistant personnel manager had told her, "and you'll learn the ins and outs of how cornflakes, perfumes, and other consumer goods are marketed. Who knows? If you have any hidden advertising talents, you might end up becoming an art or copy trainee yourself."

Unfortunately for Gabi, the creative director had taken a job at another agency after her second week at Yates, Frank, & Bingham. The man hired to replace him had brought his own secretary along, and Gabi had been transferred to a comparable position in the media department.

Gabi thought wryly about the various meanings of the word "comparable" as she stared at the pages of figures on her desk. She supposed the positions of creative secretary and media secretary were comparable in the sense that both involved typing, taking phone messages, and doing whatever other tasks were required by one's boss. But that was the end of any similarity. As a creative secretary, Gabi had typed copy for advertisements and television commercials and had regularly dealt with lively, if occasionally temperamental, art directors and copywriters. As a media secretary, she felt as if she were working in a bank. Everything she typed consisted of numbers, numbers, numbers: numbers like "cost per thousand," "price per bleed page," or "demographic distribution of readership by age, income, and ZIP code."

She glanced at her watch. It was a minute past twelve; she was already sixty seconds late for her lunch hour. Gabi took her copy of the *Swiss-American Review* from her desk drawer and slid it into her large canvas shoulder bag; her sandwich and thermos were already inside. The day was sunny enough for lunch on a bench along the Oak Street Beach, even if the weather had been cooler than normal since Labor Day.

As usual, Gabi was slightly irritated by the blatantly probing male gazes that she had to endure in the elevator. She wore no coat today, and her gold velour top above a simple A-line denim skirt revealed more of her figure than she had intended.

"I think we met when you worked in the creative department," said an expensively dressed young art director, whose leather sport jacket was of the same rust color as his hair. "Feel like getting lucky tonight? We could always meet at Ratso's."

Gabi shook her head, making it clear by her gesture that she was in no mood for the singles' bar scene. There were times when she wondered if she looked especially vulnerable, or if other young women in Chicago faced the same routine every week: a never-ending series of

6

passes from men who wanted to enjoy what they could get before disappearing from her life as quickly as they had appeared. But then, maybe she was hypersensitive —not so much nervous or prudish as unwilling to be swept along by the emotionally uncommitted, sexually restless and reckless crowd.

It was only a couple of blocks past the Drake Hotel to the underground passage that led to the Oak Street Beach. A breeze was coming off Lake Michigan, making the day feel chillier than Gabi had expected, but the sun provided a measure of warmth, as would the nylon windbreaker that she now drew from her tote. Gabi made herself comfortable on a bench that was a few dozen steps from the pedestrian tunnel. She took out her cheese sandwich on rye, poured milk into the plastic cup of her thermos, and opened the *Swiss-American Review*, which she had received in the previous day's mail but hadn't yet had time to read.

Gabi wasn't sure why she subscribed to the *SAR*, as the typographically thrifty editors often referred to their tabloid-size weekly. She supposed it had something to do with the fact that her parents had died in an automobile crash not long after her move to Chicago from the medium-sized town of Lima, Ohio. As an only child of immigrant parents, Gabi knew none of her relatives. The sisters and brothers that her parents had left behind in Switzerland were dead or had themselves emigrated to various parts of the world in the twenty years since her mother and father had left their native Bern. The *Swiss-American Review* couldn't provide Gabi with aunts or uncles or cousins, but at least it could give her a sense of having roots. Someday, she vowed, she would visit the country where she herself had been born.

Gabi skimmed the articles on Swiss business conditions, read a cooking column, and became engrossed in a piece on the problems that Swiss-Americans of different regions had when they tried to communicate in their not-always-compatible dialects. Next she read the letters-to-the-editor column and glanced at a piece on current fashions in Lausanne and Geneva. She was about to fold the newspaper and put it away when the bold headline of a small advertisement jumped out at her:

NATIVE ENGLISH SPEAKER OF SWISS NATIONALITY
SOUGHT FOR SECRETARIAL POSITION IN
CANTON BERN.

"I don't believe it!" she murmured loudly enough to elicit a curious glance from a middle-aged woman who at that moment strolled by with a large, overfed Great Dane. If the headline was almost too good to be true, the rest of the ad was no less intriguing:

Swiss author requires assistant with excellent knowledge of shorthand and a typing speed of 60 w.p.m. or better. A salary of SF 17000—will be paid, together with travel expenses to Switzerland. Interviews by appointment in New York on Thursday, September 18, and in Chicago on Friday, September 19. Send resumes to SAR, Box 61.

By now, Gabi's heart was pounding. A job in Switzerland! How she'd love to throw *that* in the face of the assistant personnel director who, in switching her to the media department, had told her that if she didn't like her new position, she could always look for employment somewhere else.

As she slipped the newspaper back into her tote and screwed the plastic cup onto her vacuum bottle, Gabi made up her mind. I'll apply for it. Why not?

She was actually smiling when she got back to the office.

Seven days later, Gabi wasn't smiling at all as she waited nervously in the foyer of a suite in Chicago's prestigious Drake Hotel. A middle-aged woman, who gave the impression of having been borrowed against her will from the hotel staff, had motioned Gabi to a straight-backed chair and told her to stay seated until the previous applicant had been dealt with.

Dealt with, Gabi thought. What a choice of words! It sounded almost as if the woman expected all of the applicants, Gabi included, to be rejected by whomever was handling the interviews on the other side of the heavy white-painted door.

Finally, after what seemed like an eternity, the door opened and an unhappy-looking girl of eighteen or nineteen pushed by Gabi without a word. "Your turn," said the woman who had earlier told Gabi to take a chair. "You're the last applicant, so I don't suppose I'll be needed any longer. Good-bye and good luck." With that sardonically delivered closing remark, the woman disappeared into the corridor.

Gabi rose from the chair and straightened up to her full five feet, one-half inch height. She had made the mistake of wearing uncomfortably high heels in an effort to minimize her shortness, and now she almost stumbled on the thick carpeting as she walked nervously into the sitting room where her interrogator was waiting for her.

"*Fräulein* Studer?" The tall man in worsted slacks and a gray tweed sport jacket stood up and surveyed her coolly with pale blue eyes, which were in stark contrast to the blackness of his neatly trimmed curly hair and the bronze glow of his deeply tanned skin. He had pronounced her name in the Swiss manner, putting a "sh" sound on the "S" of her last name. For a moment Gabi was speechless, unable to decide whether to reply in English or in German.

Her interviewer made the decision for her. "Sit down, please," he said in a cultured voice, which sounded British except for a barely discernible Swiss-German undertone. "May I offer you a cup of coffee?"

Gabi shook her head quickly, thankful that the blusher she had put on before leaving home now concealed the pinkness that crept into her fair cheeks at the sound of his resonant voice.

"Good. I would only have had to order it from room service, and there's no point in making this interview last any longer than necessary." His narrow lips turned up slightly in what Gabi assumed was a halfhearted attempt at a smile.

Gabi didn't answer. She nervously fingered the tiny Bernese coat of arms that dangled from the gold chain around her neck. She didn't know why she had worn it; maybe it was because it had been her mother's. Gabi had instinctively put on this memento of her native Switzerland before leaving her furnished room for the interview.

"I suppose I should introduce myself, Miss Studer. The name is Peter Imhof. You probably haven't heard of me,

10

but I'm reasonably well-known in the German-speaking world and have achieved a reputation among certain of the literary *cognoscenti* here in the United States." He gave another of his distant smiles. "I am, of course, Swiss. And you? You neglected to mention your citizenship on your résumé. I imagine you're another of these romantic young women who can't read an advertisement well enough to realize that an employer who specifies 'Swiss nationality' means just that."

Gabi colored. "That's an unfair accusation. Of course I didn't say I was Swiss on my résumé—I thought you'd take it for granted. After all, the advertisement was quite clear on that point."

"Yes, it was." His expression had changed slightly: His heavy black eyebrows were raised, and he looked less irritated and more interested. "Pardon me if I've misjudged you, but the last three applicants I've talked to were as American as the proverbial apple pie."

His eyes slowly scanned Gabi's face, beginning with her straw-colored bangs and moving down to her unusual green eyes with their pale lashes, which were free of mascara. Gabi reddened as he studied her small freckled nose, and she felt her cheeks grow warmer under his penetrating gaze. When his eyes moved past her narrow though full-lipped mouth to settle on the smooth throat beneath her firm if delicate chin, she couldn't help being thankful that she had worn a high-collared blouse under her jumper of salt-and-pepper tweed.

"Well," he said when he had finished examining her with his faintly mocking eyes. "You certainly *look* Swiss. All you need is to wear your hair in braids. Can you type?"

"Seventy-five words a minute, Herr Imhof."

He grinned, showing a line of straight white teeth that looked as if they could devour women stronger than Gabi. "'Mister' will do. When in Rome, do as the Romans. No doubt the same rule applies in Chicago." The grin faded, to be replaced by a more doubtful expression. "Shorthand?"

"A hundred and twenty words per minute," Gabi said with a proud upward lift of her chin.

"And to think I'd become convinced that shorthand had fallen victim to the dictating machine! Tell me, Miss Studer. Why do you want to leave your present position?"

Gabi hesitated. She knew it was considered bad form to say anything disparaging about one's current employer, but Peter Imhof clearly wasn't the sort of man who would tolerate a lot of polite nonsense. "I'm bored," she confessed after a long pause. "I type numbers all day. If I'm going to spend most of my time typing, I'd at least like to type things I might be interested in reading."

"And you think you might be interested in reading my work, is that it?" he asked a trifle arrogantly.

"I don't know. Perhaps you'd better lend me one of your published books so I can decide whether to take the job," Gabi replied with an irritation that she was unable to conceal.

To her surprise, Peter Imhof didn't seem offended by her burst of insolence. He actually laughed, and Gabi couldn't help becoming aware that his previously forbidding features took on a startlingly attractive quality when softened by an expression warmer than the distant half-smiles he had been bestowing on her ever since her arrival.

"You're rather feisty, aren't you?" he said in a tone that suggested amusement more than admiration. "You remind me of some of the girls in my creative writing classes at Bennington—minus the artistic pretensions, of course. You don't strike me as the sort who'd try to impress a man with references to Stendhal and Proust."

Gabi half-wondered if she ought to take his comment as an insult. Just because she had been forced to quit college after two years for lack of money didn't mean she was a total dolt.

Peter Imhof looked at his watch. "I suppose we had better get on with the business at hand. What would your parents say if you left the country for an indefinite period?"

"They wouldn't say anything. They died last year."

"I'm sorry." His voice carried a hint of genuine sympathy. "Were both of them Swiss, or—"

"They were born in Bern. They immigrated here about twenty years ago, when I was a year old. Mother decided that she and I should become naturalized after we'd been in Ohio for five years, but Dad was too proud to change his nationality. In any case, I never renounced my Swiss citizenship, and I still retain it as far as the Swiss government is concerned. Or so they told me at the consulate when I inquired out of curiosity after my parents' deaths."

Peter Imhof appeared to be satisfied with her reply. "Boyfriends?"

Gabi shook her head silently, reluctant to tell this man that she hadn't even had more than three or four dates since coming to Chicago. Why should she let him know how inexperienced she was with men?

"I hope you realize you won't have many opportunities to look for male companionship if you come to work for me," he said dryly. "I might add that I was thinking of hiring someone a little older and more experienced."

Gabi was about to defend her two months of secretarial background when a sudden thought made her change the subject instead. "Why look for a secretary over here? Couldn't you find one in Switzerland just as easily?"

"You've forgotten a key ingredient of my ad in the *Swiss-American Review,* Miss Studer. I specified a 'native English speaker.' Although I'm Swiss, I've spent the last four years in the United States and am fairly comfortable in both the American and British versions of the English language. I've just signed a contract for a major novel that will be published initially in English by a New York firm. So you see, I can't afford to employ a secretary who isn't conversant with the American idiom."

He crossed his legs, and Gabi found her attention wandering to the muscular thighs, which his woolen trousers outlined faithfully. "At the same time," he continued, "the secretary I hire must be Swiss because of the difficulty in obtaining work permits for foreigners in Switzerland. I'll be quite honest, Miss Studer: If you're what you claim to be, you're a godsend. I frankly didn't have much hope of finding a secretary who combined the essential qualities of Swiss citizenship and native English-speaking ability when I placed that ad in the *Swiss-American Review.*"

Gabi's pulse began to race. Surely he didn't mean—

Peter Imhof gave her another of his dry smiles. "Miss Studer, the position is yours if you want it. Now, I have to lecture three hundred students at the University of Chicago in half an hour. Can you come back at seven o'clock? We can discuss the terms of your employment over dinner."

It was a quarter to six. In her unpretentious but comfortably furnished room on Chicago's North Side, Gabi stripped off her underwear and glanced down at her naked body before putting on her dressing gown and going down the hall to the shower. She tried to see herself as a man might see her: narrow shoulders, slender waist, small rose-tipped breasts that were in perfect proportion to her trim hips and shapely legs.

Gabi turned from the mirror and slipped into her blue seersucker bathrobe. She tucked her shoulder-length blonde hair into a shower cap, since there was no time to wash and dry it properly. She couldn't help feeling an unfamiliar tingle somewhere inside her as she again contemplated what a man might think if he looked at her as carefully as she had just studied herself in the mirror. Would he see a girl, a woman, or a person who was neither one nor the other but something in between?

As she locked the bathroom door and stepped out of her robe, Gabi had to admit that it wasn't just any man who was on her mind. Her hypothetical observer was none other than Peter Imhof, if only because he had run his gaze over her so familiarly during the interview that morning. He looked like the sort of man who knew his way around women. Could it be that his experienced eyes had stripped away her garments, revealing a clear mental picture of what lay underneath?

Gabi blushed and jerked the shower curtain across the tub in an involuntary display of modesty. Why did she persist in ascribing such thoughts to her future employer? He wasn't interested in her as a woman, but had merely

15

been looking for a secretary. Any study of her female attributes had resulted from habit more than anything else. As an author, Peter Imhof was probably accustomed to making mental notes on everything he saw, just as a painter might view every landscape in terms of a canvas or watercolor.

It was five minutes past six by the time Gabi was back in her room. She quickly slipped on a pair of lemon-colored nylon bikini panties and a wispy matching bra. Panty hose were followed by a demure if close-fitting dress of undyed linen, which had a Chinese-style collar and narrow sleeves that drew attention to the slenderness of her upper arms. Gabi fastened the matching cotton webbing belt, making sure not to leave fingerprints on its polished brass buckle.

She hastily transferred her wallet, keys, and a few other essentials from her shoulder bag to a small brown leather purse. A tan trench coat with buttons that matched her handbag would offer protection against the cool breezes that evening was likely to draw off Lake Michigan.

Gabi felt a pang of nervousness when she raised her small fist to knock on the door of Peter Imhof's suite at seven o'clock sharp. What if he had changed his mind? Or what if he had simply forgotten about their appointment? A man important enough to address three hundred students at the University of Chicago might easily let a dinner engagement with a prospective secretary slip his mind.

She needn't have worried. The door opened, and Peter Imhof looked down at her with eyes that were more than a foot above her own. Gabi was taken aback. She had known he was tall, but he seemed much taller at close quarters. He seemed more overpowering, too, in his elegantly cut charcoal gray suit with a white shirt that set off his bronze tan. If only his shoulders had been a little narrower, or his jawline a bit less firm! Peter Imhof's features weren't quite handsome, but they were attractive in a harsh kind of way, and it was obvious that their owner knew it. The sardonic twist of his mouth suggested an awareness of the effect his unrelenting masculinity and his clean male scent were having on Gabi.

"You're prompt," he said dryly. "To a Swiss, that's a virtue."

"Don't forget, I'm Swiss, too," Gabi said more defensively than necessary.

"Only in the technical sense. You've spent all but a year of your life in the United States, which is why I've chosen to employ you rather than look for a more experienced secretary in Switzerland." He stepped into the corridor and checked to make sure the suite's door was locked. "Incidentally, I trust you're hungry. I've made reservations for the Cape Cod Room here in the Drake. It's noted for its fish, I'm told."

Gabi hesitated before accepting his proffered arm. "You don't need to take me to such a fancy restaurant," she said awkwardly. The Cape Cod Room was one of the more expensive dining places in Chicago.

"Let me assure you that I didn't choose it solely on your account," he answered, his words implying that Gabi shouldn't be so presumptuous. "Having come all the way to Chicago to stay in an excellent hotel, I see no point in failing to take advantage of the pleasures this hotel has to offer." He gave no sign of noticing Gabi's burning cheeks as he added, "I hope you aren't one of those midwesterners who won't eat fish unless it's tuna from a can. Let's go downstairs."

Peter Imhof's mood was businesslike to the point of remoteness when they went into the restaurant. Although he drew out Gabi's chair for her, she gathered that he did it more out of habit or good breeding than from any personal interest in her as a woman. At least he condoned her refusal of a cocktail. "It's nice to see that you don't insist on starting your meals with a glass of thinly disguised vodka or gin. Anything stronger than sherry or vermouth is anaesthesia for the taste buds," he remarked while studying the wine list.

Gabi tried to concentrate on the menu and was about to make her choice when Peter announced that he was ordering catfish. "When traveling, I prefer to sample regional specialties as often as possible," he explained. Gabi, who had been trying to decide between Maine lobster and Boston scrod, hastily settled on perch from Lake Michigan instead.

Some of the impatience seemed to drain out of Peter Imhof once the waiter had come and gone. He now smiled affably while biting into a crusty roll. "How much notice did you give?" he asked with a suddenness that took Gabi by surprise.

Gabi hastily swallowed the piece of her own roll that she had been chewing; she nearly choked on a stray crumb. "Two weeks. I forgot to ask how soon you'd need me, but I went ahead and said two weeks anyway. I can always extend my notice if you don't require me that soon."

"On the contrary. I would have preferred to have you even sooner, but I realize you can't leave your present

18

employer standing out in the cold." He gave her a seductive smile, which added a double meaning to the words "have you sooner." Gabi couldn't help wondering if he had chosen the phrase for its ability to make her self-conscious.

"Ich nehme an, dass Sie Deutsch sprechen?" His German was clearer and more elegant than Gabi would have expected from a native Swiss.

"Do I speak German? Of course," Gabi replied in her family's *Berndütsch* dialect.

"Ah! Said like a true daughter of Canton Bern. I'm surprised that your parents managed to drum Bernese dialect into you in spite of the distractions of television and high school cheerleading, but I'm grateful for their prescience. You're going to fit in even better than I had hoped."

Gabi resented his high-handed manner. "I never spent that much time watching TV, and as for cheerleading, I was considered too short to make the squad."

"Then your high school's loss was Switzerland's gain," Peter Imhof said with amusement.

"Mr. Imhof, I've been meaning to ask about living accommodations wherever we're going. Will it be hard for me to find a room or furnished flat? And will you be living in Bern proper or one of the towns around?"

"The name is 'Peter' from now on," he said before answering her question. "That sort of informality may seem odd coming from a Swiss of my generation, but I've lived in America long enough to pick up some of your habits."

Gabi couldn't help smiling at his remark. His generation, indeed! Peter Imhof might be older than she was, but he couldn't be a day over thirty-two or thirty-three.

"As to where we'll be living, perhaps you've heard of it: It's a city of thirty thousand inhabitants called Thun, and it's on the lake of the same name."

Gabi's eyes widened. Thun—pronounced "Toon"—was supposed to be one of the more impressive towns of the Bernese Oberland; it lay on the northwestern end of Lake Thun, where it met the River Aare only about sixteen miles from Bern, the federal capital of Switzerland and the seat of government in the canton, or province, that also was known as Bern. She had seen pictures of Thun in Swiss guidebooks and knew it was a small city of castles, ancient houses, parks, and views of both the lake and the magnificent Bernese Alps. Thun would be a far cry from the town in Ohio where she had spent most of her life, and it would be a sharp contrast to Chicago.

"You needn't worry about living accommodations," Peter went on. "Quarters will be provided in my house."

Gabi's fork fell to her plate with a clatter. His assumption that she would be willing to live with him left her speechless.

"Don't tell me I've scandalized you by demanding that you share my humble villa," Peter said dryly. "Though, in fact, it's hardly humble. My uncle, from whom I inherited it a few months ago, wasn't the sort of man who neglected the comforts that one can buy with wealth. You'll have a very pleasant room, and you won't have to worry about cooking for me, if that's what has you looking so alarmed. Frau Maurer, my late uncle's housekeeper, will handle the domestic duties."

Gabi thought how satisfying it would be to rap this arrogant male on his aristocratic nose. She hadn't thought about cooking for him—after all, she was to be his secretary, not his servant! "What if I don't want to live with you?" she asked with uncharacteristic sharpness.

"Then you'll overcome your dislike of the idea or withdraw your notice at the advertising agency," Peter answered coldly. "Like many authors, I'm a temperamental sort who wants to have his ideas recorded on paper whenever inspiration strikes. Since I find that my thought processes suffer when I use a pencil or typewriter, I require a secretary who will be available for dictation at all hours."

His expression thawed slightly as he went on: "Don't worry. I won't expect you to be on call twenty-four hours a day. But if you *are* in, and if I do need your services at a quarter to midnight, I'll expect you to put on your dressing gown and make the best of it. I might add that the usual Swiss work week is forty-four hours long. Yours will be much shorter—thirty or thirty-five hours at most. Putting up with my bursts of genius at odd hours on rare occasions shouldn't be that great a hardship under the circumstances."

Gabi somehow felt shamed by his explanation, though she knew that her question had been perfectly reasonable. Anyway, her objections weren't that he might ask her to take dictation before nine A.M. or after five P.M. Rather, she had been oddly intrigued by his statement that she would be living with him; but her better judgment made her question the propriety—not to mention the wisdom—of sleeping in the same house as a man like Peter Imhof. Gabi nearly blushed again when she remembered how she had reacted to the imaginary scene of his looking at her in the shower.

Her employer's challenging words interrupted Gabi's

thoughts. "We had better settle another matter before you pack up your things and leave for Switzerland, my charming Gabriele." He pronounced her name in the German way, to rhyme with "Cinderella." "The novel I've contracted to write is a modern love story, and as such it will contain scenes that may offend your virginal sensibilities. I'll expect you to transcribe whatever I dictate, even if it occasionally proves embarrassing. Is that understood?"

Gabi felt heat rush to her cheeks even as the delicate hollow of her throat became suffused with color. "I'm hardly a prude, you know. As for whether I'm a—"She didn't finish the sentence, but went on to say, "You have no way of knowing that, and in any case it's none of your business."

"As your employer. I feel that everything I can learn about you is my business," Peter replied coolly. "I can't resist adding that your reaction shows I was correct in my suspicions. There's no need to look so alarmed. A man in my position gets to know the signs."

Gabi's fingers gripped her water glass until common sense warned her to let go lest she break it. What signs? she wanted to ask, but of course she could do nothing of the kind.

"Remember, I've spent the last few years as a university professor," he added dryly. "Any reasonably present-able male who's teaching at a virtually all-female school in a small Vermont town can't help being deluged by sly suggestions from his students. It doesn't take long to learn which girls are looking for better marks, which ones are seeking more interesting relationships than they can find with boys of their own ages, and which ones are simply looking for a man who'll relieve them of the burden of their virginity." Peter lifted his wineglass in a toast. "To innocence. Unfashionable though it may be in these liberated times, it does have a certain noble charm."

Gabi didn't reply. Nor could she look directly at her new employer. In hopes of changing the subject, she asked, "When do we leave for Switzerland?"

"I'll be departing three days from now, as soon as I've given one more lecture. My belongings already have been sent ahead," he explained. "I presume you'll follow at the end of two weeks, when your duties at the advertising agency are finished. There's a Swissair flight from Chicago to Zurich; from there it's about a two-hour railroad journey to Bern. I'll arrange to meet you in Bern, since I go there regularly for shopping and research purposes."

Gabi was caught off guard. "You mean I have to get to Bern alone?"

"Surely you can find a way to cross the Atlantic without a chaperone, Miss Studer," Peter said with a formality that suggested he might already be regretting his decision to hire her. "The Swiss airline office here in Chicago can give you the particulars on how to reach Bern. I will, of course, give you enough money to cover the expenses of your journey. In fact, I'll make out a check right now."

The sum that Peter had given her was more than generous, Gabi told herself when she had tucked the check into her purse and retreated to the ladies' room before her resentment of Peter's high-handed attitude could make her say something she might later regret. For a man who dressed like a gentleman and displayed the table manners of a gentleman, Peter Imhof was anything but gentle. If only he weren't so impatient, Gabi thought irritably while splashing cold water on her hot cheeks. And if only I didn't flare up so easily in his presence!

Later, after Peter had insisted that they go for a walk along Michigan Avenue and pay a quick visit to the fashionable high-rise urban shopping center known as Water Tower Place, Gabi wondered if she shouldn't return his check and suggest that he look for a secretary after he reached Switzerland. It would be terrible to find herself unemployed in a country where she hadn't lived since her infancy.

Peter must have sensed her doubts, because he touched her shoulder gently and said, "Six months. I'll require you to stay with me that long at an absolute minimum. I will guarantee your employment for the same period, and I'll pay your air fare back to America if you decide after six months that being the secretary of a temperamental genius isn't for you." The irony with which he pronounced the word "genius" hinted at an unexpected streak of self-deprecating humor.

"Why six months?" Gabi asked, for no reason other than to hide her relief at his promise of return air fare.

"I should have the novel finished by then. I can't afford to go looking for a new secretary halfway through the book." He rested a hand on the small of her back, sending a shiver through her unaccountably tensed-up spine. "Be warned: I'll be quite merciless with you if you let me down."

"I won't let you down," Gabi said with an unaccountable pang of fear at his quietly spoken words. I'm being a fool, she thought, but there was something about the pressure of his hand on her waist that made her unable to take this last chance to decline the job.

"Very well." His voice was crisp again. "I'd better find you a taxi."

Gabi's expression froze; she had to force herself not to show disappointment. For some reason, she had assumed that he would escort her home. "That's all right," she heard herself saying from a great distance. "I can take the bus."

"Nonsense. You might be shot or strangled on the way home, and what would I do then? You're the only applicant who met my requirements." His tone seemed bantering, but Gabi knew he wasn't joking. Peter Imhof wanted her in Switzerland with him for one reason: her credentials as an English-speaking secretary who also happened to be a Swiss citizen. The knowledge should have relieved her, but in fact it inexplicably filled Gabi with disappointment and just a hint of self-pity. Did Peter really think of her as being nothing more than someone who could take his words down in shorthand and give them back in neatly typed form?

2

Seventeen days later, Gabi was leaving the Interlaken West railroad station on the last short leg of her journey from Zurich's Kloten Airport to the small Swiss city of Thun. Peter had instructed her by letter to go directly from Zurich to the capital city of Bern on an express train; from there he would drive her the remaining twenty or so miles to her new home. Gabi had chosen to ignore his letter, feeling that it was her business how she reached Thun as long as she got there on the appointed date. She had spent a night in Zurich before taking the hour-long train ride to the lovely tourist city of Lucerne for another day of sightseeing. From there it had been a scenic two-hour train ride to Interlaken in the Bernese Oberland, during which time Gabi had studied the forbidding yet beautiful shoreline of Lake Brienz as well as the Alpine peaks that looked like a row of cardboard cutouts through the high-altitude haze.

Now the electric locomotive was pulling its long line of dark green Swiss Federal Railway cars out of the station and along the southern shore of Lake Thun. The differences in geography quickly became apparent. Where Lake Brienz had offered stunning views of rocky cliffs and fogbound coves, the Thunersee impressed the visitor with its grassy, gently sloping banks and obviously sunny climate. Gabi found it intriguing that the two lakes, which were separated only by a narrow isthmus of land at Interlaken, were so totally unlike in character.

It was only a few minutes until the conductor announced their impending arrival in Spiez, the last town of any size before they reached Thun. Gabi lifted her suitcases down from the overhead rack, politely declining assistance from the young Swiss businessman who had been ogling her discreetly ever since the train had left Lucerne. She slung her bulky canvas tote over her shoulder and wished she had time to check her appearance in the washroom at the far end of the car. She had informed Peter by cable of her arrival time, and she had no reason to doubt that he would meet her at the station.

The approach to Thun was nothing short of breathtaking. As the train rounded the northwestern end of the lake, Gabi caught glimpses of forested hillsides and a chateau-like castle, which rose above red tile rooftops. Soon the train slowed down and entered the town proper; the *bahnhof,* or station, was just beyond a small canal next to the River Aare, where a pair of modern lake steamers were tied to a pier. A group of passengers could be seen disembarking from one of the large boats and walking to what appeared to be a local trolleybus station.

Gabi took a deep breath when the train came to a halt next to one of the long station platforms. She had been trying to keep images of her new employer from dominating her thoughts during the journey; her recollections of his well-tanned features, his firm manner, and the casual touch of his fingers against the small of her back filled her with trepidation and an inexplicable sense of excitement. I'll act blasé when he meets me, Gabi had promised herself, but now she wasn't so sure that she could maintain an air of indifference once she was exposed to Peter's bold masculinity. I shouldn't be going to work for him at all, she thought uncomfortably, as she tried to keep from glancing out the train window.

Manhandling her bags to the exit foyer wasn't easy, but at least the conductor was there to help her lift the heavier of her two suitcases down the steep metal steps and onto the low station platform. Gabi murmured a *"Merci vielmals,"* mingling French with German as did so many other people in quadrilingual Switzerland. Where was Peter? Surely he couldn't have failed to receive the wire she had sent from the main Zurich post office.

Gabi waited by the platform for nearly ten minutes before going into the station and asking the ticket clerk on duty if any messages had been left for a Fräulein Gabi Studer. The man shook his head, whereupon Gabi found her way to a bench and sagged nervously onto the hard wooden seat. She wondered if she should phone Peter's house or simply go there by cab.

Half an hour later, Gabi was about to look for a telephone booth when the door of the waiting room was flung open and Peter Imhof came striding toward her with an expression that showed exasperation instead of the friendly welcome she had expected. Gabi froze; Peter's grim look left her dry-mouthed and unsure of herself. She wondered if she dared say "hello."

Peter didn't wait for her to speak. Instead, he seized her

two suitcases in his muscular hands and indicated with a jerk of his head that she was to follow him outdoors. Gabi rose from her bench, reddening under the curious glance of the elderly woman who was the sole other occupant of the waiting room. She nearly tripped over the canvas tote, which had been sitting at her feet. Peter let go of one suitcase, snatched the tote before Gabi could reach for it, and tucked the overstuffed bag between his curving biceps and lean torso, which was outlined by a crew-necked pullover of brown Shetland wool. He lifted the two heavy cases as if they were filled with wadded newspaper and moved toward the door. Gabi followed empty-handed, feeling almost superfluous now that Peter had taken charge of her belongings.

A sleek red Porsche coupé of 1950's vintage was parked behind the depot. Peter stowed one of Gabi's bags in the luggage space under the hood and casually tossed the others behind the seats. He opened the passenger door for Gabi, who nervously took possession of her seat before he could change his mind and drive off without her. "Buckle up," he ordered. Gabi obeyed, wondering if she should be flattered by his concern for her safety or intimidated by his icily remote manner.

Peter slid behind the wheel. He didn't bother to switch on the ignition, but turned instead and looked at Gabi with narrowed eyes. There was a distinct edge in his normally smooth voice as he told her: "I sent you a letter instructing you to arrive on Train 128 into Bern. You chose to ignore my instructions. I suggest that you now explain why."

"I didn't really ignore them," Gabi said quickly. "I merely disregarded them."

Peter's lips twitched with what Gabi hoped was the beginning of a smile, but his forbidding expression quickly returned. "No doubt you think you have a talent for manipulating words to your benefit. Such a skill might have helped you make a career in advertising, but you chose instead to quit your job and come here as my secretary. In doing so, you obligated yourself to pay at least minimal heed to my orders."

"I don't know why it matters to you how I traveled," Gabi replied stiffly. "You said back in Chicago that I should be able to find my way here without an escort. And I did, stopping off for a little sightseeing along the way."

Peter started the engine. His muscular right hand with its sprinkling of curly dark hairs rested on the gearshift knob a few inches from Gabi's left leg. "I suppose you felt you were being thoughtful when you sent that cable advising me of your change in plans," he said with an irony that made no sense to Gabi and filled her with unease.

"It seemed like the polite thing to do." Gabi wondered apprehensively what Peter was getting at.

"Unfortunately, since I've been in Geneva for the last three days, I arrived in Bern this afternoon without knowing of your message. When you failed to get off the 3:57 train, I telephoned my housekeeper and learned that you had decided to show up in Thun rather than Bern." He aimed a scathing glance in Gabi's direction. "No doubt you'll excuse yourself by saying that late knowledge is better than no knowledge at all?"

Gabi didn't answer. She would have liked to apologize, but she was too put off by his sarcasm to do anything but sit rigidly in her seat and stare directly ahead, while her cheeks burned with humiliation from the severity of his lecture.

"Very well," he went on. "I won't belabor the issue, except to say that you're to follow my instructions in the future. I never give orders without a reason; therefore I expect my commands to be obeyed. Now, how was your trip?" This last question seemed to be a polite gesture intended to soften the harshness of his words and fulfill Peter's obligations as Gabi's host.

Gabi hesitated before replying that the trip had been smooth and enjoyable. She couldn't help being caught off guard by Peter's abrupt change in manner. Sensing that he expected her to continue, she tried to think of a non-controversial topic and hit upon the mint condition of the Porsche's interior. "Your car is beautifully preserved," she heard herself saying. "After all, it must be at least twenty years old."

"It ought to be in good shape," Peter replied as he expertly shifted gears after backing out of the parking space. "The car had only sixteen thousand kilometers on it when I inherited it along with the villa and most of my uncle's fortune. Uncle Jakob was the sort of man that we Swiss don't breed in great numbers. He was a self-proclaimed eccentric, and he regarded a sports car as being something to be driven at a leisurely pace a few times every summer, when the weather was too nice to work on his rare books collection or to play cards with his old cronies down at the local tavern."

"When did your uncle die?" asked Gabi.

"About six months ago. As the only male heir, I got the house, the Porsche, and two-thirds of Uncle Jakob's investments. A female cousin received the other third of the money as well as some of my late aunt's furniture and personal belongings." Peter paused briefly, then added: "I'm afraid Aunt Gerta is nothing but a mythical figure to me; she died shortly before I was born."

"And there aren't any more relatives?" Gabi asked out of idle curiosity.

Peter shook his head while downshifting in order to round a sharp bend in the road. "None in a position to receive an inheritance. Uncle Jakob put great stock in the idea of leaving one's fortune to firstborns. I do have a younger sister, but she's married to a prominent hotelier in Monaco who'll keep her in furs and jewelry for the rest of her days." Peter took his eyes off the road just long enough to eye Gabi carefully. "Are you taking this down? For a mere secretary, you seem unusually interested in my family and our finances."

Gabi colored. "I'm sorry. I was trying to make conversation, that's all."

"Thank heaven for small favors. I'd hate to think that a young woman of your maidenly appearance was in fact a jaded fortune hunter."

"Your advertisement in the *Swiss-American Review* was a blind ad," Gabi pointed out a trifle defensively. "It isn't as though I knew who you were when I sent in my résumé."

Peter laughed out loud. "Don't look so alarmed! I've never doubted your innocence, my tongue-in-cheek remark to the contrary. Are you so sensitive that you can't take a joke?"

It's easy for you to say that, Gabi was tempted to reply. The joke was at my expense, not yours. Wisdom kept her from giving voice to her resentment.

Suddenly a hand rested on Gabi's left arm. She looked up to see Peter looking at her sympathetically. "Now that

I think of it, your questions did sound like those of an orphan rather than those of a gold digger or potential swindler. I can see why you're interested in my family; it must be lonely to have no relatives of your own." Peter's words showed a remarkable degree of understanding. Gabi wondered if this was his way of apologizing for his unfair accusation without losing face.

Gabi's concern about Peter's opinion of her faded as they rounded the point where the River Aare split off from the lake. Though it was a cool day in early October, half a dozen sailboats could be seen against the backdrop of shoreline, foothills, and snow-covered mountain peaks. "It's beautiful!" Gabi cried exultantly.

Peter turned left just before they reached another settlement along the banks of the Thunersee. "That's Hünibach up ahead," he said. "You'll find several guest houses there, and of course many of the local people rent rooms to tourists by the day or week. It's a common practice in Switzerland, even among the middle classes."

They climbed a winding road, which led upward toward Alpine meadows. "Goldiwil is above us," Peter went on in his best tour guide's manner while pulling over to let a yellow Swiss postal bus go by at alarmingly high speed. "It's primarily a farming settlement. I'm sure you know that dairy farming plays an important role in the Bernese Oberland's economy. Vineyards and orchards are also common around Lake Thun, since the climate is so mild. Believe it or not, figs are actually grown here even though we're sitting at the foot of the Alps."

A gravel road marked *"Privat"* led off from one side of the road and disappeared into a screen of trees. Peter downshifted and turned onto the drive. A moment later, Gabi blinked at an unexpected burst of sunshine as the

Porsche emerged from the cluster of spruce and drew to a halt in front of a magnificent chalet built of dark wooden shingles and heavy timbers in the timeless Bernese Oberland style.

Gabi was rendered speechless by the rustic beauty of the three-story house with its vast overhanging eaves and its steep foreroof, which was broken by a semicircular wooden arch. Each of the tall, narrow multi-paned windows had a box of geraniums beneath it; an ornately carved second-floor balcony ran the full width of the house's façade.

"I don't suppose it looks much like your last place of employment," Peter said dryly as he opened the car door for Gabi.

Gabi stepped out of the Porsche and onto the lush meadow grass that grew on either side of the unpaved drive. "All I need is an office with a window," she answered lightly. "Then I'll have a better view than any of the vice-presidents at Yates, Frank, & Bingham."

"You'll have an office with several windows, although honesty compels me to add that you'll be sharing it with me. And the view ought to be more dramatic than you'd get from the average skyscraper, since my humble *schali*, as a chalet is called in these parts, is nearly a thousand feet above the lake."

Gabi inhaled deeply. The scent of hay and manure added a tang to the fresh, crisp air. She could see cattle and a farm tractor in a meadow higher up on the hill, which was mostly forested but had a number of large clearings. "Don't tell me you're a dairy farmer in addition to being a writer?"

"Not really. I do own some farmland in the vicinity, but

it's leased out. A dog is my only concession to animal husbandry."

A dog! Gabi had always been fond of dogs, but she hadn't had one of her own since the family cocker spaniel had died when she was in junior high school. "Has your dog been here all along, or—" Gabi's question was interrupted by the deep bark of the Old English sheep dog that flew out of the chalet's front door as if summoned by their conversation. An elderly woman emerged a few seconds later and came toward them without haste. She wore a scarf around her head and had a white cotton tunic over her baggy dress of dark, nondescript cotton. *"Gruezi,"* she said, addressing both Peter and Gabi in the traditional Swiss manner.

Gabi returned the jerky Swiss handshake with the smoother American equivalent. She learned that this was Frau Maurer, who had been housekeeper to Peter's Uncle Jakob for many years and now took care of Peter's meals and other domestic needs. The dog was named Winifred and had been acquired during Peter's four-year stint as a professor of creative writing and German literature at the prestigious "Seven Sisters" college of Smith.

"So! Bitte kommen Sie herein!" Frau Maurer said in a heavy local accent. Gabi followed the housekeeper inside while Peter took her bags from the car.

Gabi had no time to look into any of the rooms that opened off the main entrance foyer. Frau Maurer led her directly up the heavy wooden staircase to the second level, where contemporary paintings and modern wall hangings lent touches of color to the long hall with its floor of varnished wood.

"Ihr Zimmer, Fräulein," said the housekeeper, swinging a door open and gesturing with a gnarled hand. Gabi stepped into the room and was immediately taken aback by its size and by the simple but elegant modernity of its peasant-inspired furnishings.

The room was far larger than the cramped servant's bedchamber Gabi had half-expected. Three windows afforded an astonishingly lovely view of the woods and meadows that spilled down the hillside toward Lake Thun; one could even see the villages on the lake's southern shore.

The three-quarter-size bed, dresser, and wardrobe were made of a heavy native pine stained to a golden hue. The bed had a goosedown *decke,* or duvet, buttoned into a sheet sack of bright green cotton, which was printed with tiny white wildflowers. The highly polished floorboards complemented the paneled walls and were in turn set off by a colorfully patterned Scandinavian rug in a tight woolen weave. A small writing desk had its own bentwood chair of the classic Austrian Thonet design, while a double-cushioned sofa upholstered in a nubby cream-colored wool faced the windows. There was even a little round table with two more bentwood chairs next to the French doors that led to the balcony.

Frau Maurer told Gabi in German that she could wash up and come downstairs at her leisure. Gabi went into the hall and found the bathroom, which was equipped with ultramodern fixtures of bright orange ceramic with a matching medicine chest. A full-length mirror was hung in one corner next to the separate tub and shower. Gabi noticed that her denim skirt was wrinkled from the long hours of sitting on the train. Oh, well; she could always change clothes later, after Peter had delivered her luggage.

Peter was just setting her bags down when Gabi returned to her room. "I hope you find your quarters satisfactory," he said with one of his inscrutable expressions.

"Oh, yes. My room in Chicago was comfortable enough, but this is much larger and cheerier. And it'll be nice to have a balcony."

"The balcony won't be of much use when winter comes," Peter told her. "Still, if our arrangement lasts into the spring . . ." He didn't finish the sentence, and Gabi tried not to react to the various meanings implicit in the word "arrangement." Theirs was to be a business relationship, she told herself firmly. She would have to learn to stop blushing like a schoolgirl every time Peter made a double entendre at her expense.

Gabi stepped to the window and looked at the gently curving shores of Lake Thun. "What's that big castle-like building off toward Interlaken?" she asked in hopes of keeping their conversation on safe ground.

"It's precisely what it looks like—a castle. It's called Schloss Schadau, and it's open to tourists during the summer. Perhaps I can arrange for us to visit the gardens before the flowers are gone for the season." Peter looked at his watch. "I suggest that you have a shower now and be downstairs at half past six. Frau Maurer has indoctrinated me into my uncle's lifelong habit of early dining. No doubt you'll be hungry after your long day of traveling and sightseeing."

Gabi wondered again if Peter was criticizing her subtly for having come on the train via Lucerne instead of going

directly from Zurich to Bern. If so, that was his problem
and not hers; what she did on her own time was her
business and not her employer's.

She quickly unpacked her bags, took out her toilet kit
and robe, and headed for the bathroom. The water in the
shower was hot, the soap smelled of mountain herbs, and
the huge towel that she used for drying off afterward was
warm from its heated rack. Gabi folded the towel neatly
and glanced at her nude body in the full-length mirror.
Her skin was flushed from the invigorating shower, and a
few glistening droplets of water still clung to her softly
rounded curves. She wondered, not for the first time,
what it would be like to stand before Peter with nothing to
shield her body from his appraising gaze. This mental
picture made Gabi feel vaguely apprehensive; her fantasy
was all too likely to become reality if she didn't keep her
mind off her employer's male attractions. As though to
ward off temptation, she turned quickly away from the
mirror and reached for her underwear.

Peter was removing the cork from a bottle of Swiss
wine when Gabi found her way into the rambling
wohnstube. The living room had walls of dark pine; its
floorboards matched those in her own room, and all of
the sofas and easy chairs were upholstered in soft leather
that was the color of milk chocolate. One wall was
bisected by the traditional tile stove and chimney. A
modern open fireplace of rough stones occupied the far
corner of the L-shaped room, while the area nearest the
entrance door was dominated by a large grand piano
with a lacquered ebony finish. A rectangular oak dining
table stood next to wood-framed plate glass doors that
opened onto a flagstone terrace behind the house. The
table was already set for two. Gabi, who wasn't used to

servants, had expected Frau Maurer to eat with them, and she casually said as much.

Her host looked amused by her remark. "Frau Maurer would be scandalized by the idea of dining with us," he said as he poured a glass of chilled white wine for Gabi. "We Swiss are quite democratic—more so than any other people, perhaps—but our traditions of service preclude the kind of informality that one takes for granted in the United States."

Gabi took the proffered glass of wine with some misgivings. She wasn't used to drinking alcohol, partly because her parents had been abstainers, but mostly because anything more than a glass of white wine or champagne made her feel drowsy. And so, when Peter touched her on the shoulder and suggested that they proceed to the dining area, she naively credited her unfamiliar sensations of pleasure to the sip of wine she had just swallowed. She wondered vaguely if her new employer were trying to ply her with alcohol before leading her upstairs to see his collection of etchings. I'm being silly, she told herself, and she vowed to maintain a cool, sophisticated demeanor even as her heartbeat sped up when Peter helped her with her chair.

To her relief, Peter made no attempt to exploit her awareness of his disconcertingly physical magnetism during dinner. He was the perfect host, explaining that the roast chicken was called *mistkratzerli* and that the greens in the salad had been picked fresh that evening from a garden on the hillside above the chalet. He questioned Gabi about her knowledge of Swiss cooking and seemed disappointed that she hadn't sampled much beyond the inevitable fondues and, in Zurich, a supper of veal bratwurst with *rösti*, or shredded potatoes, fried to a golden crispness with a touch of onion. "We'll have to broaden your horizons," he said firmly. "I'll have a word with Frau Maurer after you've settled in."

Dessert was a tray of cheeses served with fresh fruit from the Italian-speaking Swiss canton of Ticino, called "Tessin" by the Germanic Swiss. Frau Maurer brought in large cups of black coffee brewed in an espresso machine from dark beans, which she had ground by hand only moments earlier. A healthy dose of scalded milk and generous quantities of sugar made the rich beverage more acceptable to a palate that was used to a weak midwestern brew.

After Frau Maurer had cleared away the dishes, Gabi made a point of offering to help with the washing up. Frau Maurer rejected the suggestion with a horrified smile, which caused Peter to laugh tolerantly. "If Frau Maurer ever lets you into her kitchen—and I suppose she'll have to, since it's where we eat breakfast—then you'll see her array of modern labor-saving devices. Come—let's retire to the living room, and I'll let you try some of the local kirsch."

Kirsch, also known as *kirschwasser*, was a brandy distilled from cherries. Gabi had heard of it but hadn't ever sampled any. She wasn't eager to try it now, and she politely said so.

"It's part of your Swiss heritage, and I insist that you try it at least once," Peter replied. "You needn't have it again if you find that you don't like it."

Gabi knew better than to argue with Peter. She accepted the thimble-sized glass of clear liquid with the dubious expression of someone who was being forced to hold a spoonful of unfamiliar medicine.

"*Prost,*" her host said cheerfully, lifting his glass and

tossing back its contents with no visible ill effects, as he sat next to Gabi on the couch.

Gabi decided it was time to demonstrate her own sophistication by foregoing the cautious sipping approach. If Peter found the kirsch harmless, so would she. A quick breath to gather her courage, a jerky movement of her fingers followed by a backward snap of her neck, and—"Oh!" Gabi felt as if someone had applied a blowtorch to the roof of her mouth. Her throat was burning, hot fumes were spreading through her nasal passages to the farthest reaches of her head, and her eyes were beginning to water from the shock of gulping three-quarters of an ounce of high-proof alcohol. She felt a light-headedness sweep over her, and only fast action by Peter kept her from slipping sideways onto his lap.

"I could have warned you that might happen," Peter said with quiet amusement as his strong hands took hold of Gabi's trembling shoulders.

"Then why didn't you?" she rejoined, her heart beating wildly from the effects of the kirsch and the surprise of feeling Peter's fingers pressing into the flesh of her arms through the soft sweater.

"And miss the pleasure of coming to your rescue? Nonsense." His tone was light, but there was an undercurrent of something more portentous that made Gabi want to twist from his steady hold.

"Let me go," she breathed.

"Don't be silly. You'd only strike your head on the floor or coffee table. I'd be saddled with an on-the-job injury claim before you'd begun working for me."

Work. The word shot through Gabi's consciousness almost as sharply as the kirsch had done. Tomorrow she would be working for this man, sitting in his office and listening attentively while he dictated the opening pages of a novel. From the way Peter had toyed with her so far, she wouldn't be surprised to find him making up the most outrageous kind of sex scenes, scenes that he had no real intention of using, just so he could amuse himself by watching her reactions.

The sharp scent of Peter's after-shave lotion served as a tantalizing warning that his face was now next to hers. Gabi opened her eyes, which she had closed briefly while trying to will away the effects of the kirsch, and she saw the hard line of Peter's jaw only inches from her own.

"I'm very pleased with life in my uncle's chalet," Peter murmured, his breath warm and seductive against Gabi's cheek. "I have an excellent view of the Jungfrau from here."

Gabi stiffened. In addition to being the name of the famous mountain that faced Interlaken and Lake Thun, *"jungfrau"* was the German word for "virgin." How dare Peter make fun of her that way!

"I fear I've miscalculated," he continued in a bantering tone. "I thought I had you under my spell, and look! I've only made you angry."

"I'm not angry," Gabi snapped back, but her words were belied by the obvious resentment in her voice. She looked away from Peter before he could see her discomposure. Why on earth had he brought up her lack of sexual experience again? Gabi's mind flashed back to their dinner in the Cape Cod Room, where he had first made reference to her "virginal sensibilities." She wondered if Peter were the sort of man who got pleasure out of toying with innocent young women before robbing them of their virtue. Not that virtue really had much to do with virginity; in her case the temptation to sleep with men had always been more abstract than real.

Peter's right hand unexpectedly grazed Gabi's cheek, the slightly callused fingertips generating a spark of pleasurable sensation as they trailed across her delicate skin and moved down to explore the curve of her jaw. Gabi parted her lips to murmur a protest; no words came out. Peter's forefinger began to stroke the hollow behind her ear. Her anger had gone now, to be replaced by an exquisite shyness that forced her to look away lest Peter see the emotion that his touch had wrought within her.

Gabi was taken completely by surprise when Peter's face appeared in front of her own and his lips settled firmly on her trembling mouth. Her sharp intake of breath was cut off by his kiss; Gabi panicked and tried to push him away, but her hands thrust against his muscular chest to no avail. Peter's kiss, cool at first, took on a more forceful quality as Gabi reeled under his naked assault on her senses. This can't be happening, she told herself, but the reality of the probing kiss was echoed in the pounding of her temples, the constriction in her chest, and the unfamiliar yet welcome feelings that were being sent like tiny jolts of electricity to every sensitive nerve ending in her body.

She was like a ship torn from its moorings, a bird tossed from its nest, a child uprooted from the safety of a familiar environment. When Peter's lips freed themselves from her mouth to apply gentle pressure to the throbbing pulse in the hollow of her throat, Gabi's head fell backward in an unwitting gesture of abandon. His mouth moved from her throat to her neck; she sighed as she felt his closely shaven whiskers against her skin. It was the touch of sandpaper on satin, of woolen tweed against soft velvet, and it forced Gabi to surrender the last of her inhibitions with a deep shuddering moan. Phrases like "I can't," "he daren't," "we shouldn't" floated across Gabi's consciousness and were immediately submerged by the rising tide of her desire as she felt a hand move inside her blouse to stroke her nipple into aching hardness. Her initial responses quickly gave way to deeper, more profoundly erotic sensations; feelings so intense that they sent a tremor of need through her body, feelings that provided a foretaste of sensual ecstasy even as they stole her breath away.

It was Peter who, in the end, drew back and spoke the words that brought their unplanned lovemaking to an abrupt halt. "If you're to remain a *jungfrau,* my sweet, we'd better avoid melting what's left of your glacier."

Gabi went rigid from the insult and bit back a sharp rejoinder. A glacier! He had no business making fun of her that way, especially after the way he'd led her so far in so short a time.

"I'm sorry," Peter said in the wry tone that she found so infuriating. "It was a turn of phrase that I couldn't resist. We writers are like that, you know—anything to show our mastery of the language."

Only of the language? Gabi thought bitterly, but she kept her words to herself. She sat up with a rather forced primness and tugged her skirt over her knees. "I've had a long day," she murmured in what she hoped sounded like a calm voice. "I'd better be going to bed."

"Yes." Peter's tone carried no expression. Gabi looked to see if he might secretly be laughing at her, but his face was as inscrutable as his reply.

The walk to the staircase seemed to last a lifetime. Gabi

was conscious of Peter's gaze on her back, uncomfortably certain that he was appraising her legs, her hips, and her proudly held shoulders with the unemotional gaze of a connoisseur. Had the whole episode been planned? Or had Peter simply taken advantage of her moment of weakness before his awareness of their employer-secretary relationship had brought him to his senses? There was no way to know, and Gabi certainly didn't have the nerve to ask.

She made her way upstairs a little shakily while trying to find some logic in Peter's oddly contradictory behavior. He had shown himself by turns to be cold and passionate, harsh and tender, businesslike and kind. What sort of man lived behind the array of masks? It was impossible even to guess. Gabi knew only that she had never met a man quite like Peter Imhof. She vowed not to let him take advantage of her inexperience; if he ever broke through her defenses and ravaged her body with the same degree of mercilessness that he occasionally showed in his role of employer, she would be an emotional wreck by the time her six-month trial was over.

3

Gabi felt awkward when she walked into the kitchen the next morning. Peter was already at the breakfast table, and he appeared to be engrossed in the morning newspaper. Gabi expected him to look up from his *Neue Zürcher Zeitung* with a sly smile or some other veiled reminder of what had taken place the previous evening. To her surprise, he did nothing of the kind. He merely shoved a basket of fresh croissants toward Gabi and said that Frau Maurer would be happy to serve her café au lait or cocoa, whichever she preferred.

"*Kaffee, bitte,*" Gabi said to the elderly housekeeper, who already had begun to scald a pot of milk with high-pressure steam from a small but elaborate-looking espresso machine. Gabi turned her attention to the rolls. They were light and flaky, and she spread one of them with unsalted butter from an earthenware crock. Frau Maurer brought the separate pots of coffee and hot milk to the table as Gabi was spooning jam onto her breakfast plate.

Gabi and Peter ate in silence for several minutes. For Gabi, the meal was turning into an ordeal. She had slept badly the night before in spite of retiring early. Part of today's exhaustion was due to jet lag, no doubt, but several hours of tossing and turning in an unfamiliar bed hadn't helped any. If only Peter hadn't kissed her! His unexpected embrace had made Gabi feel as confused and worried, as pleased and frightened, as a fifteen-year-old girl who had been kissed a little too expertly after her first date.

Finally, Gabi could stand it no longer. The issue had to be brought out into the open and dealt with honestly. If Peter had been toying with her, so be it; a forthright statement of his casual intentions would at least put their new employer-secretary relationship into the proper perspective.

Gathering all her courage, Gabi set down her coffee cup and stared at the back of Peter's newspaper. "Excuse me." She knew her voice sounded weak and a little shaky, but there was nothing she could do about that.

"Yes?" Peter responded politely, lowering his newspaper to look her in the eye.

Gabi was flustered by his seemingly impersonal gaze. "About last night . . ."

"There's nothing to talk about." Peter went back to the article he was reading. A moment later he folded the newspaper, put it aside, and began spreading fruit preserves on a croissant.

"I hope you don't think I'm in the habit of succumbing to men's advances," Gabi went on in an embarrassed tone. "I was tired. I had a glass of wine at dinner—I'm not used to it, you know—and after you talked me into trying that kirsch . . ."

"I said there's nothing to discuss." Peter sounded impatient now, and Gabi looked down at her coffee cup

47

to hide her humiliation. Why was Peter refusing to hear her out? Was it because he considered the whole matter unimportant? Gabi recalled his words back in Chicago about the students who had thrown themselves at him in Vermont. Did he think she was using the wine and the kirsch as an excuse for abandoning her conscience with an attractive male who also happened to be rich? If only I hadn't accepted this job, she told herself numbly. Now it was too late to back out.

Peter rose from the table and left the kitchen without another word. Gabi glanced quickly at the housekeeper, who was already coming to clear away Peter's dishes. Frau Maurer's expression told her nothing. Gabi wondered if the woman had detected any of the tension between Peter and herself. At least Frau Maurer didn't appear to speak English; this was something to be thankful for whenever there was any possibility of an embarrassing conversation with Peter.

After leaving the kitchen and brushing her teeth, Gabi went upstairs to the office, which doubled as the chalet's library. Peter wasn't there yet, so Gabi contented herself with a careful inspection of the room, which took up the entire top floor of the chalet.

The office was impressive, far more so than the sterile if expensively decorated offices assigned to the top executives of Yates, Frank, & Bingham in Chicago. Tall windows along the chalet's façade offered a view comparable to that of her bedroom, while the windows on the back wall overlooked the hillside behind the house with its meadows and forest. Sloping ceilings at either end of the room led down to vertical walls, which were completely covered with bookcases. Some of the shelving was old, while other portions were of more recent vintage. A glimpse at the books on the shelves revealed a fairly even balance between aged leather-bound volumes and modern books in cloth or paper bindings.

Peter walked into the room while Gabi was examining an ancient rough-hewn table that looked as if its timbers had been shaped with an adze. "Don't tell me you're a fancier of antiques?" he asked, startling her.

Gabi hastily straightened up and snatched her hands from the table. "Not really. But I do like old things."

"I'll have to remember that in another forty years," Peter said mysteriously, and Gabi had no time to draw any inferences from the remark as he continued, "You may be interested to know that this table was made by my great-great grandfather who lived just a few kilometers from here. He was a farmer, and I suspect that he made this table with the same tools that he used to cut firewood."

Peter rested a hand on Gabi's shoulder and drew her toward a modern Danish-style desk with an L-shaped typing extension. "Here's your desk. I bought the typewriter last week. It has a built-in memory and an electronic display above the keyboard that shows the last few words you've typed, so you can correct errors before the machine commits them to paper." His fingers slid lightly down Gabi's upper arm before returning to his side. Gabi shivered, and Peter scrutinized her with a casual air of amusement. "Forgive me. Did I touch a nerve?"

Gabi shook her head, unwilling to risk an answer.

"You'll pardon my reference to errors, too, I hope," he added in a tone that Gabi, in her defensiveness, interpreted as being mocking. "I don't suppose you allow yourself to make many mistakes."

Only big ones, like taking this job, she was tempted to respond. Her better instincts forced her to keep the rejoinder to herself. Instead, she made an innocuous and rather inane comment about the number of books in Peter's library.

"This is nothing compared to what you'll see in a few months," Peter answered with the pride of the true bibliophile. "Many of these books are from my uncle's collections. I have another dozen crates of books on their way here from Vermont." His right arm snaked out to take Gabi by the shoulder. "You might want to sit in the armchair while I give dictation; I prefer to pace the floor or put my feet up on the table you were admiring so fervently when I came in."

Gabi hastily stepped out of his loose grasp and moved to the leather-upholstered chair beneath the small glass skylight. She had already found an unused stenographer's pad, and she now took out her fountain pen.

Peter's manner became more businesslike when he saw that Gabi was ready to work. "Very well; we might as well start in. Today we'll do the opening section of the first chapter, which has been outlined in detail and which I've already 'written,' in a manner of speaking, in my head. I'll dictate until the spirit leaves me, whereupon you can begin transcribing your shorthand. If you could, I'd like you to type a neat draft of the material after lunch. I'll make corrections this evening before I retire, and you can file the corrected sheets until I'm ready to have you type the completed and fully edited manuscript next February or March."

Gabi's nervousness gave way to a feeling of confidence, or at least competence, once Peter's dictation was under way. He had a surprisingly rapid-fire dictating style in comparison with Gabi's former bosses in Chicago. No doubt this reflected the fact that the novel was already "written" in his mind and didn't require him to do a lot of thinking on his feet, Gabi told herself as her pen flew over the lined sheets of her steno pad.

It wasn't long until Gabi found herself becoming interested in the chapter's content. The opening scene was a conversation between a professor and the wife of his college's president. The two were discussing the professor's short-lived affair with the woman's daughter, and it was obvious to Gabi that the woman was making a play for her daughter's former lover.

Gabi tried not to become too interested in the material, but she couldn't help noticing that the scene was witty and fairly racy in a highly sophisticated sort of way.

Suddenly, to her horror, Gabi realized that she had lost track of her place. In allowing herself to pay attention to the dialogue she was writing down, she had missed at least a paragraph of dictation.

"Excuse me—" She bit her lip, breaking off the sentence when Peter looked at her quizzically. Then, after a short hesitation, she continued. "I'm afraid I've lost my place."

Peter nodded and closed his eyes. "Read back what you last wrote down," he commanded. Gabi obeyed, and Peter managed to pick up the scene where Gabi's shorthand had left off.

All went well until Gabi became distracted by a callous remark made by the professor to his ex-girlfriend's mother. Gabi looked up sharply, and when her eyes returned to the steno pad, she discovered that she had again missed several lines of dialogue.

Peter, who had been glancing in her direction from

time to time, suddenly noticed that her pen was being held motionless above the lined tablet. His eyebrows lifted sardonically. "Lost again, Miss Studer?"

Gabi colored and nodded without a word.

"Try to concentrate on the words, not the story," he said with thinly disguised impatience. "You're here to take dictation, not to exercise moral censorship over my characters' behavior."

Gabi inhaled sharply. "How dare you speak to me that way?" she blurted.

"My dear Miss Studer—"

"Gabi," she said stubbornly. "It was your idea to use first names."

"Very well. Gabi. And let's not have any nonsense about what I dare or dare not do. The freedom to do and say as I please is one of the reasons I became an author. Presumably you didn't enter the secretarial profession because you were looking for independence or the chance to assert yourself at will."

Gabi's temper flared. "Then perhaps I made a mistake."

"Perhaps you did indeed," Peter replied coolly, "but it's a bit late for second thoughts. You agreed to stay here for six months. We both have a job to do; I shall do mine, and you shall do yours. I suggest that we carry on with our respective duties, starting now. Next paragraph. . . ."

It was after eleven when Peter announced that Gabi could put away her steno pad. He must have noticed that she was tired, because he looked at her sympathetically and remarked, "I hope I didn't work you too hard on your first day; although, when I hired you, you didn't strike me as the type of person who was afraid to give value for payment received. In that respect you're different from some of the secretaries I've had."

Gabi smiled at the unexpected compliment. "And have you had so many different secretaries?" she asked in an impulsive burst of curiosity.

"A few." Peter gave a little laugh that was as disconcerting as it was pleasant-sounding. "In a college town, one inevitably has to hire students to do secretarial work. The work ethic hasn't exactly blossomed in the current academic generation, and in any case it's hard to get much accomplished when a secretary regards her employer as a potential lover or—worse yet—as a prospective husband."

Gabi didn't answer, but merely prayed silently that he hadn't noticed the color which had begun to darken her cheeks for no good reason.

"Fortunately, Mary Cleaver arrived to save me from a legion of calf-eyed students who could neither spell nor type."

"Mary Cleaver?" Gabi echoed, hoping for more details.

"Mary was the wife of a young assistant professor of anthropology," Peter explained in a matter-of-fact tone. "Joel Cleaver was in Africa for a year, traveling in rustic circumstances with a tribe of nomads while gathering material for a book. Mary had a great deal of time on her hands, and I was able to capitalize on her loneliness by offering her a job."

"I see." Gabi's reply was uncertain; she didn't see at all.

"It wouldn't be accurate to say that Mary was the

perfect secretary. She wasn't very good at shorthand, and she didn't speak German as well as you do, but she had other talents that compensated for any minor skills that she lacked. She gave willingly of herself, asked little in return, and never showed signs of wanting to latch onto me for life as some of her younger predecessors did."

Gabi nodded wordlessly. Was Peter trying to imply anything when he referred to his ex-secretary's "other talents"? And what exactly had Mary Cleaver given while asking for little in return? Her time? Her body? Or both? The more Gabi thought about it, the more suspicious it all sounded, even though it was always possible that any wrongdoing existed only in her own mind.

"Enough of my past relationships with secretaries," Peter said, his unexpectedly sharp voice breaking into Gabi's troubled thoughts. "You might as well start transcribing the material I've dictated this morning, unless your fingers are too tired. I'll tell Frau Maurer to expect you for lunch at noon."

"Where are you going?" Gabi asked without thinking. "Aren't you eating lunch here?"

Peter's eyebrows lifted in surprise, and Gabi wilted as he looked at her. "I hardly think my plans for lunch need to be submitted to you for approval," he said with what Gabi took to be sarcasm.

"I'm sorry. I didn't mean it that way. Tell me—will you be dictating any more today, or shall I plan to concentrate on my typing this afternoon?"

"That's it for the day, unless my muse makes an unexpected reappearance after lunch." Peter's tone had become friendly again in a cautious way, as if he realized that there was little point in their getting off on the wrong foot during the first day of working together. Gabi found herself thinking that it was too bad he had incurred her disapproval with his talk of past secretaries and especially of his relationship with the one who had been married. In his less distant moments, he seemed almost likable, even though the impression of decency that he sometimes gave might be nothing but a façade.

Gabi felt a pang of something—sadness, perhaps, or a trace of envy—when Peter left the library to go off on his luncheon date. Though the morning had been marked more by tension than by companionship, she had enjoyed working with him after the boredom of her job in Chicago. There was something rather exhilarating about taking dictation from a respected writer like Peter Imhof and knowing that his words—words which were likely to outlive their author—were being committed to paper for the first time by her, Gabi Studer. It was a little as though Picasso or Renoir had handed her a palette and brush and told her to apply his mental brush strokes to a sheet of canvas. How much more rewarding this sort of work was than typing up media schedules for deodorant ads and cornflake commercials!

As she transcribed the morning's dictation, Gabi made penciled marks next to several idioms that sounded a little too British to her American ear. The most glaring inconsistency appeared in the dialogue of the dean's Southern wife: "How could you be so cruel as to treat my daughter like a common tart?" The word "tart" was more likely to be used by an English dowager than a faded Southern belle, and Gabi thought the error should be brought to Peter's attention.

Frau Maurer was setting a place at the dining room table when Gabi emerged from the stairwell a few minutes before noon. "Oh, please! I'll eat in the kitchen with you," Gabi said in Bernese dialect when the housekeeper motioned to the chair she had occupied the night before.

The elderly woman ignored Gabi's request, and her expression was so forbidding that Gabi didn't dare press the matter. Gabi felt awkward sitting alone at the long table with Frau Maurer serving her *salées au fromage,* or cheese cakes, along with hearty onion soup and a glass of white wine. It was too bad that Peter hadn't remained in the house for this, her first lunch at his chalet. Gabi wondered where he was eating this noon, and with whom. When Frau Maurer returned with a cup of strong *kaffee,* Gabi tried to make conversation by asking if this was a typical Bernese-style lunch.

The housekeeper shook her head. "In Switzerland we eat our large meal at noon and have sausages or cheese or *birchermuesli* at night. Herr Peter has learned to follow the English and American habit of a light luncheon and heavy supper." A smile crinkled the woman's weather-beaten features. "It is easier for me, because I do not have to get up so early to prepare dishes that require hours to cook," she added in her harsh-sounding Swiss German.

Gabi incurred Frau Maurer's disapproval by carrying the soiled dishes to the kitchen after finishing her meal, but she refused to be intimidated by the housekeeper's protests. "I'm not a guest; I'm an employee as you are," she told the woman firmly. She was tempted to add that Frau Maurer was treated less as a servant than she was, if

56

Peter's behavior that morning had been any guide, but she kept her opinion to herself. If there's one thing I'm learning in this job, it's to hold my tongue, Gabi thought wryly on her way upstairs to the library.

The morning's dictation was completely transcribed by two o'clock. Gabi found an empty file cabinet and began to set up a file for the as-yet-uncompleted manuscript. She wondered if she should also arrange a correspondence file, but it was possible that Peter already had a workable system for storing and retrieving his business letters. She would have to discuss her clerical duties with him later on, when he had time to show her the contents of the packing boxes labeled MANUSCRIPTS AND CORRESPONDENCE which she had found in a closet at the top of the stairs.

By three o'clock, Gabi had run out of things to do and was trying to kill time by inspecting the German and Swiss magazines which were neatly stacked in one of the bookcases. She didn't feel much like reading. After nearly a day in the chalet, she felt the need to become more familiar with her surroundings. A walk would be pleasant. Surely Peter didn't expect her to hang around the office until four-thirty or five o'clock with no work to do. Frau Maurer was perfectly capable of taking any phone messages.

Gabi went to her room to fetch a light windbreaker. She then told Frau Maurer that she was going outdoors for an hour or so. As she headed uphill on a narrow path that led toward the woods, she heard a noise behind her and turned to see Winifred, the sheep dog, trotting up with her tongue hanging out in an expression that was utterly disarming. Gabi bent down, tousled the sheep dog's furry ears, and continued up the path with the large bear-like creature at her side.

It was a perfect day for exploring the meadows and forest above the chalet. The air was surprisingly warm for early October, and Gabi soon had the windbreaker tied loosely around her waist in order to let the sun beat down on slender forearms that she had exposed by rolling up the sleeves of her plaid cotton blouse. She was wearing jeans and lightweight hiking boots; her hair was tied back with a rubber band, which she had taken at the last minute from her desk drawer to save the bother of finding a headband among her still unsorted belongings. I'm hardly a fashion plate this afternoon, she told herself when she stopped to admire a trio of cattle wearing large brass bells, who were grazing at the far end of the meadow. Not that her appearance really mattered; there was no one to see her but the cows and Winifred—unless, of course, a herdsman emerged from the woods to offer the inevitable *"gruezi."*

It was well after four o'clock when Gabi suddenly realized that she had hiked much farther than she had intended. Frau Maurer might be wondering if she had become lost in her new and unfamiliar environment. Besides, the sun was already beginning to drop behind the trees, and Gabi's muscles were becoming sore from the unaccustomed exercise. She wasn't used to hiking uphill after the unrelieved flatness of Chicago's parks and sidewalks.

Gabi felt decidedly sweaty and grubby when she reached the chalet at a quarter past five. She patted Winifred, who had stopped to drink from a trough near the barn-like garage, and went to the house alone.

Voices were audible through the half-opened door to the living room when Gabi stepped into the foyer. One voice was Peter's; the other was a woman's. The two were conversing in *Berndütsch*. Gabi heard the voices break off as soon as she had closed the front door behind her. She was about to go upstairs and wash when Peter opened the inner door and beckoned her into the living room.

Gabi instinctively raised a hand to the rubber band that she had used to tie back her hair. "If you don't mind, I'll have a shower first," she said apologetically. She nearly added that she wasn't quite sure what her place was in the social scheme of things anyway, since she was an employee and not a guest in Peter's household. Maybe it would be better if she stayed in her room until Peter's visitor was gone.

"Nonsense. You can wash up later," Peter said with more forcefulness than charm. "I want you to meet Ilse."

Gabi began to move toward the staircase, but Peter caught her wrist in an iron grip before she could get away. When she tried to pull her arm free, he increased the pressure on her wrist. Gabi reluctantly gave in to his persistence and allowed herself to be led into the living room like a shy and rather antisocial child.

Ilse turned out to be a strikingly beautiful young woman with hair the color of anthracite coal. The thick tresses piled atop her head glittered blue-black from a careful application of lacquer. On anyone else the coating of hair spray would have looked cheap or old-fashioned, but on Ilse it created a geisha-like effect, which was in lovely contrast to her pale, clear skin and her almond-shaped eyes whose irises were the shade of bitter chocolate. Gabi wondered how old Ilse was. She guessed twenty-seven or twenty-eight; the girl had a sophisticated look that hinted at experience in dealing with men of the world like Peter.

Ilse looked at Gabi while raising her carefully sculpted brows in a silent but meaningful question.

"My secretary, Gabi Studer," Peter said with American-style informality. "Gabi, meet Ilse Delacroix."

Gabi merely nodded. She wasn't surprised by the French surname, since she knew that Bern had a large French-speaking minority and was on the border between the German- and French-language regions of Switzerland. Somehow the name seemed appropriate to Ilse, who would have looked more at home in a Paris salon than in a *bierstube* or the barn of a Bernese dairy farmer.

Ilse touched her elaborately coiffed hair in a gesture that seemed calculated to display her shapely bosom to best advantage. Her other hand rested on a smoothly curving hip, and one leg was thrust out ahead of the other in a pose that reminded Gabi of a photograph in *Vogue* or *Harper's Bazaar.* Gabi suddenly became aware of an expensive scent, which was in sharp contrast to her own sweaty aroma. Had Peter forced her into the living room in an attempt to remind her of how inadequate she was next to women like Ilse Delacroix? If only I hadn't stepped into a pile of cow manure and been forced to crawl under a barbed-wire fence, Gabi thought as the heat rose slowly in her cheeks. I must look and smell like a cow.

"How unfortunate that you weren't able to join us for lunch," Ilse said with cool courtesy. "I'm sure you had the time, since it appears that you don't find it necessary to work as long or as hard as secretaries whose employers require them to keep normal office hours." Ilse's English was faultless; she spoke with the assurance of one who felt equally at home in Los Angeles or London, Newcastle or New York.

Gabi was about to offer a rejoinder when Peter interceded smoothly. "I'm sure Gabi had her work finished before she went on her hike," he said with a wink in Gabi's direction. "She's very conscientious, even if she does react unfavorably to my racier bits of dialogue."

Ilse's eyebrows again lifted condescendingly. "Surely there isn't too much shocking material in Peter's new book?"

"It's too early to tell. I've only read the first scene in chapter one," Gabi said in a tone that barely concealed her dislike of this patronizing woman. She decided to go upstairs before she said anything she might later regret. "If you'll excuse me, I really do need a shower."

"Of course," said Ilse. Her voice implied: Yes, you really do, don't you? Gabi fled the living room with clenched fists and flaming cheeks.

Gabi spent more than half an hour in the bathroom and her bedroom, hoping Ilse would have gone by the time she came downstairs in a clean dress. Alas, her hopes were dashed when she returned to the living room to find Ilse taking a sip from a glass of wine that Peter had just poured for himself. Ilse's own glass of a darker wine was sitting on the buffet. It appeared that Ilse was planning to stay for dinner.

"Would you like to try some of this?" Peter asked,

taking his glass from Ilse and holding it out for Gabi. Seeing the way Ilse looked at her, Gabi blushed and shook her head. "Don't be antisocial," Peter said dryly. "Here—I'll pour you a glass of your own." Gabi accepted the fresh glass of wine reluctantly, unhappy with the amused and rather superior smile that played across Ilse's lips.

Dinner was excellent, but Gabi got little enjoyment from the food because she was so displeased with the company. Ilse behaved as if she owned the chalet. Gabi had heard of guests being invited to make themselves at home, but Ilse gave orders to Frau Maurer as though she were already Peter's wife. Was the icy, elegant Ilse destined to become the future Frau Imhof? Gabi wondered, but she didn't dare ask.

The conversation turned to Peter's late Uncle Jakob when they had coffee in the living room. Peter noticed Gabi's surprised reaction to Ilse's use of the word *onkel* and apologized for having failed to give more detailed introductions earlier. "Ilse is my cousin," he explained to Gabi. "She lived with Uncle Jakob in the last months before his death."

"I see." Gabi felt reassured without quite knowing why. Unfortunately, her relief turned out to be short-lived.

"You failed to point out that I'm your second cousin, not your first cousin," Ilse said sweetly and with a look that made the unspoken message perfectly obvious. "Your new secretary may as well understand the true nature of our relationship, dear."

Peter laughed, but his laugh was tolerant and not at all pleasing to Gabi under the circumstances. Gabi tried not to show her dismay; Ilse's barely discernible smile soon told her that her attempt had failed. She was grateful when Frau Maurer cleared away the coffee cups, thereby making it easier for her to plead a headache and withdraw once again to the privacy and loneliness of her room.

4

~~∞∞∞∞∞∞∞∞∞~~

The next day began as the previous morning had, except that Peter was not at breakfast. Gabi was buttering a roll and wondering if he were up yet when he walked into the kitchen and told Frau Maurer not to bother preparing lunch.

Gabi looked at her watch. It was already past eight-thirty. "Shall I expect you upstairs later than usual?" she asked her employer.

"Not at all. I've already breakfasted. I'll be in the library as soon as I've had a shower." As he turned to leave the kitchen, Gabi noticed that he was wearing the same shirt he had worn the night before. Could it be that he had stayed overnight at Ilse's house or apartment, eating breakfast there before returning to the chalet? The possibility was enough to kill Gabi's appetite. She knew she had no real basis for her suspicions, and that Peter might well have put yesterday's clothes on to take an early morning hike; but she couldn't help feeling a pang of jealousy as she thought of his spending the night or even a few pleasurable moments in Ilse's arms.

Peter arrived in the third-floor office just as Gabi was

filling her pen. His hair looked damp, and he was wearing a plaid woolen shirt above a pair of form-fitting corduroy trousers that emphasized his virility. Gabi found herself noticing the dark curly hair that was visible through the open collar of his shirt. Before she knew it, her mind was forming an involuntary and vividly realistic image of Peter standing in the shower. She reddened and forced the disconcerting picture from her thoughts. Her blush became even deeper when she saw Peter looking at her oddly, and she was grateful when he didn't ask the reason for her embarrassment.

The morning's dictation went smoothly. Gabi made it a point to keep her mind off what was in Peter's novel, concentrating instead on taking the words down as they came. If she wanted to think about Peter's dialogue and character descriptions, she could do so later on while transcribing the material.

She did interrupt Peter a few times to question specific grammatical usages and idiomatic expressions. Peter appeared to be less than pleased the first time Gabi questioned a minor error of syntax, but he soon developed a respect for her editorial talents. "You're going to be even more useful than I thought you'd be," he said when Gabi caught him using an Americanism in a slightly awkward way. "I thought I had your language down flat—"

" 'Pat,' " Gabi corrected.

Peter tilted his head in a mock bow. "I beg your pardon. 'Pat.' It's clear that I overestimated my grasp of the finer nuances. Having you to second-guess me will prevent foolish errors that would only make things harder for my American editors."

They reached the end of the first chapter shortly after

eleven o'clock. As Gabi got up from the armchair and moved toward her desk, Peter intercepted her and laid a hand on her arm. Gabi sighed instinctively, unable to control her purely physical response to his seductive touch.

"How long will it take you to type up the material I've just dictated?" Peter asked, seemingly oblivious of the effect that his fingers were having on her.

"No more than an hour and a half." Gabi wondered what the hurry was about.

"Good. When you've finished, I'll take you into the city, and we can have lunch there. Then we'll shop and enjoy the sights."

Gabi was surprised and pleased. When Peter had told Frau Maurer not to worry about lunch, she had assumed that he would be lunching in town with Ilse or some other acquaintance and that she would be left to fend for herself. He must have been secretly planning this excursion all along. It showed an aspect of his personality that she hadn't known existed: a sensitivity to the needs of others and a generosity that was in pleasant contrast to his sometimes arrogant and demanding behavior.

Gabi had the remaining pages of the first chapter typed by half past twelve. She changed from her denim skirt and checked cotton blouse into a lightweight woolen skirtwaister that bore a passing resemblance to Donegal tweed. The day was pleasantly cool, so she added a rust-colored suede blazer that she had bought with some of the vacation pay she had received when leaving her job in Chicago. Chocolate-brown stockings and a pair of Italian sandals completed her sightseeing outfit.

Peter gave her a capsule history of Thun as they drove along the lakefront road. "The town dates back to the

Middle Ages," he explained. "The Dukes of Zähringen pretty much owned the city of Bern in those days, and Thun was one of the places they annexed in building up their regional empire. Eventually another Bernese dynasty, the Kyburgs, took control of the town and the castle above it. The nobility are long since gone, of course. Switzerland was one of the first countries to turn its back on the concept of a titled aristocracy; maybe that's one of the reasons why we were producing merchants and dairy farmers when royal courts in Germany and Austria were turning out the likes of Beethoven, Haydn, and Mozart." His tone became wry. "Democracy has its virtues, but I can't help thinking that any wealthy and reasonably educated nineteenth-century nobleman probably did more for music and painting than all of today's government arts committees combined."

They had lunch at the Hotel Krone on the *Rathausplatz*, or City Hall Square. Gabi hadn't felt terribly hungry upon being seated in the Krone's dining room, but she quickly developed an appetite when a delicious-looking asparagus omelette and *pommes frites* were placed before her. The omelette had a delicate golden crust on the outside and was runny on the inside; the French fries were the best she had ever tasted. Gabi had no objections when Peter suggested that they have *vermicellis*, spaghetti-like noodles made from pureed chestnuts, for dessert.

After lunch, Peter took Gabi up a covered set of outdoor stairs to Schloss Thun, the castle which overlooked the town from a steep hill that rose from the main business district. The castle was a dramatic sight to someone used to the more modern buildings of Chicago. Its rectangular central portion had only a few deeply set windows below the sharply pitched roof; four circular towers made of the same neutral stone thrust toward the sky with pointed roofs covered in tile. A tile-topped stone wall meandered down the hillside, broken here and there by beautifully preserved watchtowers.

"How do you like our local castle?" Peter asked when they had climbed to the top floor and made their way to one of the windowed corner turrets.

"It's fantastic," Gabi replied truthfully. "And the setting is enchanting!" She let her eyes rove over the trees, gardens, and vineyards below. "It's almost pastoral directly beneath us, yet the shops and hotels are only a few steps away. We can go from the Middle Ages to the twentieth century in just five or ten minutes. In Chicago I used to think a building was old if it was built before 1920."

"As long as we're here, we might as well take a look at the museum," Peter said when Gabi had taken her fill of scenery, which included the lake, the mountains in the distance, the twin branches of the River Aare, and the town itself.

The Knights' Hall with its array of tapestries was magnificent. The historical museum's display of traditional Bernese crafts and utensils was fascinating and made Gabi more aware than ever of her own Swiss heritage. She vowed to return to the Schloss Thun on her own, so that she could examine the various domestic exhibits at her leisure without having to feel that she was taking up too much of Peter's time.

It was after three o'clock when they had left the castle. Peter told Gabi that he had to pick up some groceries for Frau Maurer before they went back to the chalet. "If you'd like, we'll window-shop along the Hauptgasse on our way to the supermarket," he said.

Gabi found the Hauptgasse, or Main Street, interesting because it had two levels of storefronts, the higher being built on the side of the castle hill. The doors of the upper shops opened onto a second-story sidewalk, which was built on the roofs of the stores below. Wrought-iron railings were enhanced by flower boxes and an occasional potted palm, the latter a curious sight in this region but not really surprising in view of Thun's mild climate.

Soon they were in a large supermarket, one of a chain of stores which were to be found all over Switzerland. "The larger supermarkets sell washing machines and other household appliances," Peter explained to Gabi. "Some of them have camera departments and other specialty counters, and many of the stores have full-fledged restaurants as well."

Gabi was surprised to find that most of the foods came in very small packages. One exception was breakfast cocoa, which was available in huge 2.2-pound bags. Even the milk was packaged in nothing larger than a liter carton. When Gabi commented on this, Peter explained that the Swiss often bought their milk at bulk prices in a *molkerei*, or dairy shop, bringing their own miniature milk pails with them.

Gabi insisted on carrying some of the groceries when they finished their shopping. This left Peter with one hand free, and he rested it lightly on Gabi's waist as they walked back down the Hauptgasse to the street where the car was parked. Gabi was curiously elated, yet at the same time worried, by the gentle pressure of Peter's fingers on her hip. Did he make such gestures every time he strolled with a woman? Was he trying to give her a subtle message, perhaps a hint that he wanted to make love to her? Was he amusing himself at her expense? Gabi stole a glance at Peter's face but learned nothing from his enigmatic expression.

They passed a young couple who were embracing in front of a jeweler's window. An engaged couple wondering if they could afford a diamond, Gabi thought enviously. She wished she could share in the girl's obviously carefree feelings. Gabi wasn't in a hurry to get married, yet she looked forward to the thrill of planning a wedding. Maybe I should count myself lucky that I've never been faced with any real temptation, Gabi told herself before recalling in a flash that this was no longer true. Peter had tempted her as much as any man could tempt a woman; the fact that she had emerged unscathed did credit to his self-control and not her own.

As if in response to the lovers' presence, Peter's fingers tightened on Gabi's waist. Gabi was startled. She began to move away, but Peter's hand pulled her gently toward him. She looked at Peter and saw an amused smile play across his lips.

"Don't," Gabi said sharply, jerking out of his grasp. She wasn't angered by his squeeze; she resented only what she read as condescension.

"You weren't objecting when I touched you a minute ago," he said mildly.

"That was different."

"Different? In what way?" he asked with lifted eyebrows and another of his infuriatingly arrogant smiles.

"You were being . . . oh, I don't know . . . 'impersonal' is the word I'm looking for, I guess."

70

"And you let men caress you impersonally? I thought virgins were more careful."

Flames of humiliation engulfed Gabi's cheeks. "Will you stop talking about my virginity?" she blurted.

"I don't recall mentioning it since we were in Chicago. Perhaps it only seems that I've been talking about it because you've been so busy thinking about it," Peter suggested.

"I'd forgotten all about it until you brought it up."

"Good. Maybe you'll forget about it again when we get back to the chalet. We aren't having company this evening, and I can think of better things to do than play cards or watch television."

Gabi felt his hand touch her hip again, and she jumped forward. "You're insufferable!" she cried, the scarlet of her cheeks darkening to crimson when an elderly by-stander cast a startled look in their direction.

"You only call me insufferable because you're afraid to suffer the consequences of my attraction for you," Peter said with a playful gleam in his eyes.

"You have no attraction for me," Gabi lied.

"Then why did you have such a dreamy expression on your eminently readable face when I touched you the first time?" he asked with indisputable logic.

"Because . . ." Gabi sighed. What could she say? Her feelings must have been transparent. Still, she had to give some sort of an excuse. "I was homesick," she said lamely.

"In that case, we'll go home." Peter took Gabi by the arm and led her across the street to the Porsche. Gabi felt a little as if she were in the hands of an abductor when he opened the passenger door and motioned for her to get in. Soon they were on their way back to the chalet. Peter hardly spoke during the trip, and Gabi was too furious with him and with herself to make idle conversation. She was grateful when Peter asked her to take the lightest bag of groceries into the house while he deposited the car in the garage.

A polite truce existed between them during supper. Gabi made small talk about the *hafersuppe,* an oatmeal soup enriched with potatoes and Emmentaler cheese. She expressed her delight in the *kalbsbraten,* veal that had been roasted with minced vegetables and bacon before being served with tiny dumplings called *hörnli.* Dessert was a tart of sliced pears and ground filbert nuts. When Gabi asked what flavorings were in it, Peter remarked that she was displaying a surprising interest in Swiss cookery for someone who was a career girl rather than a homemaker.

"Just because I'm a career woman now doesn't mean I'm not interested in cooking," Gabi retorted, putting the emphasis on the word "woman." "I don't want to limit my options for the future."

"Surely you don't intend to become a career *man* instead?" Peter's expression was deadpan, but there was a note of humor in his voice.

"That's not what I meant."

"No, but it's what you implied. Dramatic inflections shouldn't be used by people who are unable to employ them properly," Peter told her in the manner of an English teacher chastising a careless student.

Gabi's fingers curled instinctively against her place mat, but she managed to keep her temper under control.

"I suppose you meant to tell me that you planned on

having a husband and children someday," he said, still enjoying himself.

"I'm not planning anything. But it does sound like a nice idea," Gabi conceded.

"And where do you expect to find this sire for your offspring?" Peter asked musingly. "Not in Thun, of course. Swiss males may not be as chauvinistic as the Greeks or Italians, but I doubt if they're boyish enough for your American tastes."

"I'm as much Swiss as American," Gabi pointed out.

"Legally, perhaps. Culturally, you're a product of your environment, and I recall your saying that you left Bern when you were a year old."

Gabi didn't answer. She wasn't ready to admit that he might be right.

"Let's go back into the other room." Peter slid his chair back and rose from the table. "I don't suppose you play a musical instrument?"

She shook her head. "I played the cymbals in my high school band, but I haven't touched them since graduation."

"Cymbals don't lend themselves to parlor music in any case," Peter said dryly. "Come. I'll play you a polonaise."

Peter sat down at the aging but well-preserved Blüthner grand piano and applied his fingers to the keys. "What a pity that you don't play the violin or the piano. We could have tried a duet. Still, perhaps you're a good listener." He launched into a forceful but fluid interpretation of Chopin's *Polonaise-Fantaisie*, closing his eyes and playing entirely from memory.

Gabi was intrigued, if somewhat disconcerted, by this

aspect of Peter's personality. She hadn't realized that he could play the piano; after all, the old Blüthner might have been in the house for years. In any case, she would have expected him to lean more toward Beethoven or possibly even one of the moderns rather than a purely Romantic composer like Chopin.

She found herself wondering if he had ever had dreams of playing professionally. His talents were obvious; his interpretation of the polonaise had a strong, masculine quality that one often didn't hear with Chopin. Come to think of it, there probably wasn't anything surprising in the quality of his playing. Peter had an air of ruthless self-assurance that undoubtedly encompassed nearly everything he did.

Does he perform like this for Ilse? she wondered. Gabi felt an unaccountable pang of jealousy, until she realized that Peter hadn't had much time to get into the habit of doing anything with Ilse. Peter had been in this house only two weeks longer than Gabi herself. On the other hand, a lot could happen in two weeks, especially when two people had known each other as long as Peter and Ilse presumably had. Gabi reminded herself that Peter was in his early thirties, and Ilse was only four or five years younger, so both of them had had plenty of time to become intimate before Peter went to Vermont for his teaching stint at Bennington.

Gabi's speculations about Peter and Ilse were interrupted when her employer closed the fallboard of the piano and asked if she cared for an after-dinner liqueur.

"No, thank you," Gabi said without hesitation. "I don't like hard liquor, and in any case I had a glass of wine with dinner."

"How about a tiny glass of *alpenbitter*, a specialty of

the Appenzell region in eastern Switzerland?" he persisted.

Gabi tried to stop his hand when he reached for a bottle inside the drinks cupboard. "The name alone is enough to discourage me," she warned.

"Try it before you make a judgment." Peter poured out a thimble-sized glass and handed it to Gabi. She screwed up her courage, took a tentative sip, and made a horrible face as the liqueur's bitter aftertaste overwhelmed her tongue. Peter chuckled. "If you find it that offensive, you'd better wash away the taste with peppermint schnapps." He poured out a larger shot of clear liquid, which Gabi accepted without demur. Gabi caught a whiff of a cool, refreshing aroma and had to concede that the peppermint schnapps would be a useful antidote to the *alpenbitter.*

At Peter's toast of "To your health!" Gabi forced down a generous mouthful of minty spirit. She choked for a second or two before becoming enveloped by a warm, relaxed feeling that didn't go away, even when her host led her to the couch and sat down beside her.

"I take it that your inhibitions are being dissolved by the alcohol?" Peter asked in a gently teasing tone.

"A little," Gabi admitted with more honesty than she might have shown under normal circumstances.

"Then perhaps you'll give me a frank opinion of the novel you've been typing for two days now. What do you think of it so far?" He sounded genuinely interested in hearing Gabi's opinion, and this surprised her.

"I'm not sure what to say," she replied. She considered herself a secretary, not a literary critic.

"Come now. You must have drawn some conclusions from the opening chapter."

Gabi put down her empty glass. "Well, I guess I was a little taken aback at first by the hero's behavior with—" She hesitated, unsure whether she should finish the derogatory remark.

". . . his girlfriend's mother?" Peter prompted.

"I'd hardly call her a 'girlfriend.' That term suggests affection. I got the impression that the professor was merely using the girl for . . ." Gabi's voice trailed off in an uncharacteristic display of reticence.

"Yes?" Peter asked with raised eyebrows and a twisted smile.

". . . for his physical gratification," Gabi finished.

"And you don't think affection and physical gratification can go hand in hand?"

Gabi shook her head. "I know it's fashionable nowadays to talk of sex between 'friends' that involves no emotional commitment, but I don't believe there's any such thing. Sex can be an accompaniment to love. Or it can be carried out impersonally to relieve physical tensions, as a sailor might do on shore leave." Gabi looked Peter in the eye. "People who say they can make love casually and be good friends afterward are only deceiving themselves."

"I take it that you've acquired that rather firm opinion through personal experience?" Peter asked dryly.

Gabi bridled. He's trying to make a fool of me, she thought, though she had to concede that she had brought it on through her own air of self-righteousness.

"And how do you feel about the alternative to love?" Peter continued. "I refer, of course, to sex as a means of relieving physical tensions."

"I find it a tragic waste of something that should bind

people together in a lasting and loving relationship," Gabi replied.

"You're quite certain there isn't any way you could respond to a man's attentions without being in love with him?" Peter asked with an odd glint in his eyes.

"Of course!"

"In that case, let's test the power of your convictions." Before Gabi could react verbally, Peter was taking her into his arms. She tried to pull away but felt herself being crushed against him until she was gasping for breath. Peter boldly took advantage of her parted lips by kissing her with an unyielding yet somehow tender assertiveness. She resisted initially, but was soon clinging to him with an ardor that she was unable to suppress.

"Peter! Please!" Gabi tried to plead between kisses, but her moan was to no avail. She became aware of her reluctance being stripped away in a torrent of exquisite sensation wrought by the intense probing of his kiss. Gabi was filled with a painful longing to have Peter caress her with the same intimacy. It's the alcohol, she told herself during a lucid moment, but the gnawing ache in her loins refused to be quelled by last-minute rationalizations. She wanted to open herself to him; she longed to have him destroy her innocence once and for all with the virile strength that she had sensed in one of his previous embraces.

Just when Gabi was about to beg Peter to stop tormenting her and move on to the next stage, he took his lips from her own and gently pushed her away. His passion seemed to have faded, and she noticed that he was contemplating her with an expression that suggested clinical interest rather than sexual need.

"So. Either you love me or you're one of those tragic women who settle for raw physical satisfaction," he said calmly.

Gabi's knees were trembling; her skin felt as though it were badly sunburned, hot as it was from his touch. "You planned that, didn't you?" she accused in a shaky voice.

"Only on the spur of the moment. You were being so arrogant in sounding off on matters you knew nothing about that I couldn't resist bringing you down a notch."

"You're nothing but a beast!" Gabi cried.

"Look at yourself in the mirror, *Liebchen*. You fall into that classification yourself, to judge purely by your animal responses."

Gabi, almost as infuriated with herself as she was with Peter, jerked down the hem of her skirt before rising unsteadily from the couch and going to the window. She wouldn't flee this time, she decided; she would stay and behave as though nothing of consequence had happened. If he could maintain his equanimity after such unrestrained passion, then so could she!

5

~~~~~~~~~~~~~~~

Gabi went upstairs to bed earlier than usual, but it didn't take her long to realize that sleep wouldn't come easily. How could she relax and settle down for the night after what had transpired in the living room?

She unlocked the French doors and stepped onto the balcony. The Thunersee was almost black this evening except for patches of silvery reflections where the waters caught the moonlight. Gabi's eyes drifted to the shoreline and the twinkling lights of the villages on the lake's far side. She inhaled deeply; the cool night air smelled of farms and forest, grass and livestock. It was hard to imagine a more peaceful setting. Yet the war between the sexes was being waged here, in this chalet, with Peter having won every battle so far. Would it always be so? Was she destined to spend the next six months feeling as though she were nothing more than the spoils of war to be enjoyed by a conqueror named Peter Imhof?

If only I'd had more experience with men like Peter back in the States, Gabi told herself as she turned and stared through the glass doors into the warmth and brightness of her room. How welcoming that bedroom looked! Last night, upon fleeing Peter and Ilse, she had looked upon it as a place of refuge. Now she knew it was no such thing: It was merely a comfortable cell in which to bide her time until Peter took it upon himself to advance their relationship toward its inevitable conclusion. If I had any sense, I'd leave now, Gabi thought. Yet how could she leave? She had made a promise to stay six months, and if she did leave she would be breaking that promise and opening herself to whatever ruthless form of revenge Peter might take. He had warned that he would show no mercy if she let him down. I'm a prisoner, Gabi decided bitterly—a prisoner of my own foolishness and desire.

Desire. How odd the word sounded when applied to herself! Gabi had never felt desire before, except for the vaguest and most innocent stirrings of the sort a girl might experience when being kissed by an attractive escort after the junior prom. To Gabi, desire had always suggested warmth and comfort and affectionate snuggling. Now she recognized it for what it actually was: trembling, aching, the tantalizing pain of wanting to cling to a man's hard, demanding body. Her brief acquaintanceship with Peter had taught her a great deal about the relations between men and women—more, perhaps, than she was ready to face.

Gabi let her gaze wander to the lake again. She thought how far she had come in such a short time. Some five thousand miles from Chicago to Zurich, followed by several hours of railroad travel to a chalet on the shores of Lake Thun. Yet in her heart and in her body's knowledge of itself she had traveled even farther: from ignorance to awareness, from contentment to a nagging emotional ache that left her all too vulnerable to another person's control.

She found herself wondering again if Peter's decision to hire her had been based on ulterior and not-altogether-respectable motives. Had he really intended that she come to his chalet only to help him with his new book? Or had he paid her way to Switzerland for that reason but also to add spice to an otherwise quiet rural existence?

I'm imagining things, she told herself firmly. She had no real grounds for being suspicious of Peter; surely a man of his rugged good looks and sophisticated charm had no need to hire a woman to provide him with late-night entertainment, especially when his lovely and fawning cousin Ilse was so close at hand. Still, he had warned that as a creative person he was subject to bursts of inspiration. Who could say that he wasn't just as easily seized by physical impulses that drove him to look for satisfaction at odd hours of the day or night? Gabi had to admit that Peter might find it convenient to have a secretary in his house and at his beck and call, and not only to take shorthand—providing, of course, that there were no two-sided romantic entanglements to complicate their business relationship during working hours.

A click behind her made her stiffen. When she looked around, it was to see Peter emerging from a pair of French doors at the other end of the balcony. He was wearing a rough woolen robe in a dark tartan plaid whose colors Gabi couldn't make out in the shadows. Gabi felt a twinge of excitement when she noticed his strong, bare legs and slippered feet.

"I thought you were retiring for the night," Peter said before stopping a yard from Gabi to rest one elbow on the balcony railing.

"I will, in a while. The fresh air was tempting."

Peter studied Gabi as though she were some unfamiliar species of wildlife that needed careful observation to see whether it might be tamed. "You're an intriguing woman," he said after a while.

Gabi colored. "I can't imagine what you mean."

"It's really quite simple. On the one hand, you become very stiff at the slightest hint of scandalous behavior—say, between the characters in my novel. On the other hand, you respond to my caresses like an experienced and willing partner until something—I assume it isn't merely your conscience—hangs out a warning flag. Can you explain that?"

Gabi couldn't tell if his tone was sincere or mocking. She decided that her best course of action was to ignore the question altogether.

"Well?" he asked when the silence had become uncomfortable for Gabi.

"I—I don't know what to say."

Peter shrugged. "It really doesn't matter, so long as we're both sensible enough not to become trapped in some deep involvement that might jeopardize our working arrangement. Which brings me to another point: I must confess that I've overstepped with you a few times." His teeth showed in a wolfish grin. "Tonight you more or less challenged me to kiss you when you took up arms for moral decency and virtue."

"And you don't believe in decency and virtue?" Gabi countered accusingly, stung by his implication that she might be falling in love with him.

Peter made a vague gesture. "I have my own definition of both. It isn't quite so narrow as the one you profess to believe in. But then, I always take great pains to avoid being hypocritical."

Gabi's temper flared. "Are you saying that I'm a hypocrite?"

"Your responses when I kissed you hardly reinforced your image as a *jungfrau,*" he pointed out with a hint of amusement.

"You're cruel!" She lifted a hand impulsively and sent it flying toward his cheek.

Peter deflected the smack with an automatic movement that seemed almost contemptuous by its very ease. "Honesty is never cruel. On the contrary, it's an act of mercy to those who require a confrontation with the truth to bring them to their senses, *Kindli.*"

Gabi froze at what she took to be a mocking diminutive. "I'm not a child."

"Not when you're giving yourself up to the joys of lovemaking, anyway." He grinned again, this time with a frankness that made Gabi look away in shame. "You only act like a child when your temper gets the better of you. But to return to what I was saying earlier: Let's remember who we are and why you're here, and we'll both be saved from a potentially awkward situation."

Gabi was almost too furious for words. At long last she managed to grind out a rejoinder: "You needn't worry. My only interest in you is a professional one. I wouldn't let you get me into bed if you asked me to marry you."

"Good." Peter's voice was now curt to the point of harshness. "Both of us would do well to keep that in mind in the future."

* * *

Gabi's next encounter with Peter began awkwardly. Still, he didn't comment when she blushed as she asked him to pass the rolls at breakfast, and by nine o'clock Gabi was ready to concentrate on dictation rather than on what Peter had said the night before.

Peter was absent for lunch and wasn't very talkative at supper. When he did speak to Gabi, it was in a remote manner. Somehow this new behavior pattern didn't strike Gabi as being convincing, but she supposed she ought to be grateful that he was trying to keep her at arm's length. There was no telling what might happen if he gave in to boredom or simple physical lust and imposed himself on her after Frau Maurer had gone up to bed.

He played a work by Mussorgsky on the piano after dinner. His technique was virtually faultless, and his interpretation left Gabi deeply moved by his sensitivity to what the composer must have been trying to say. If only Peter were more sensitive to her own feelings! Gabi longed to change his new impression of her. She wanted to tell him again that she believed in romantic love, that she felt uncomfortable about the idea of sex before marriage no matter how her body had betrayed her when she was in his arms. It's your fault that I responded anyway, she wanted to point out. How could you expect me to be indifferent? You're an experienced lover who knows all the tricks of the game, while I'm a virgin who doesn't know how to defend herself against a man of your ruthlessness.

On Saturday morning, Gabi came down to breakfast to find Peter getting ready for a trip. "I'm off to Zurich for a meeting of a Swiss literary awards committee," he explained when he saw Gabi's quizzical glance. "I'll be back on the train late Sunday night. Frau Maurer will ask what you'd prefer in the way of meals while I'm gone."

At first Gabi was almost relieved to see him go. He had made it clear that weekends in the chalet would be reserved for relaxation, not work, and the thought of being alone in his presence without the buffer of work was intimidating after their recent conversation on the balcony. The realization that Peter might spend most of his Saturdays and Sundays with Ilse didn't make things easier for Gabi. She knew she had no right to be jealous of Ilse; she nevertheless couldn't help envying the other woman's knack for making herself at home, not only in the chalet, but with Peter.

Gabi spent the morning washing her lingerie, blouses, and jeans in the modern washer-dryer located in a roomy pantry off the kitchen. Frau Maurer had already tried to take over Gabi's laundry chores, but Gabi had remained insistent about doing them herself. "I used to haul everything to the laundromat in Chicago," she told the housekeeper, "so I find it no great hardship to bring my washing down one flight of stairs."

It didn't seem particularly strange to have lunch without Peter; he had been absent several times at meals during the previous week. Gabi began feeling restless by early afternoon, however. She wandered into the kitchen and engaged Frau Maurer in a conversation that resulted in her learning that Ilse lived only a couple of kilometers away. Gabi made a quick decision. She would go on a walk and see how the other woman lived. The house might not say a great deal about its owner, but it might reveal at least a few intriguing tidbits about its owner's personality.

She took Winifred along for company. For the first time, she noticed the bright red leather heart dangling from the sheep dog's collar. Gabi had seen similar hearts on dogs in Zurich and Lucerne; no doubt they were identification tags of some sort. A snapped-down flap at the top of the heart suggested that a tiny ID card might be inside. The heart stood out nicely against Winifred's gray-and-white coloring; Gabi decided to buy one and mail it to a friend back in Chicago who had a Labrador retriever.

Today she and Winifred followed the road downhill toward the lake. A gravel track led off the asphalt road about fifteen minutes away from Peter's house. Turning left, Gabi walked past a farm and a cluster of trees until she reached half a dozen modern chalets, which appeared to have been designed by the same architect. From Frau Maurer's description, she knew that the one on the far right was Ilse's.

There was nothing distinguished about the chalet. It was small, well-kept, and surrounded by a modest garden with a bench facing Lake Thun. A short gravel driveway extended along one side of the house and was occupied by a bright red Italian roadster. The shutters were open, but the curtains at the windows were closed, even on the lower level. Gabi had the impression that no one was at home.

For some reason the thought that Ilse was away from the chalet bothered her. If Ilse was in town shopping, why would all the curtains be closed? It looked almost as though Ilse had gone away for the weekend; perhaps she had been collected by someone else since her own car was in the drive. Could she have gone to Zurich with Peter? A sense of foreboding stole over Gabi as she paused a dozen yards from the chalet's entrance path and stared at the curtained windows. Had the committee meeting in Zurich been an excuse for a weekend spent among the cosmopolitan attractions of a city much larger than Thun? Or—and this was more likely—had Ilse learned of Peter's scheduled trip to Zurich and invited herself along so he wouldn't lack feminine company? A vaguely sick feeling raced through Gabi's abdomen. The latter ploy seemed exactly like the sort of trick that Ilse might use.

Gabi turned and began walking toward the main road. She was barely conscious of Winifred's happy panting at her side. I have no business thinking about a possible affair between Peter and Ilse, she told herself. If anyone were an interloper, it was she; Ilse had arrived on the scene first.

Sunday dawned warm and clear, unusually so for this late in October. Gabi felt restless as she breakfasted on the American-style cinnamon rolls that Frau Maurer had surprised her with when she had come downstairs after her morning toilet.

"They're good, aren't they?" asked Frau Maurer in German. She had begun nibbling on one of the rolls herself while peeling carrots for a stew.

"*Wunderschön.*"

"*Von Amerika,*" the housekeeper went on, explaining that Peter had obtained the recipe from a female acquaintance in Vermont.

Gabi nodded, hoping that her curiosity about the "female acquaintance" wasn't too obvious. The recipe wasn't the only thing Peter had brought with him from America, she added silently. He had hauled along a naive young secretary, too. Gabi was beginning to wonder why Peter found her less appealing these days than he did the recipe for cinnamon rolls. Granted, she was probably safer being left alone, but she couldn't help wishing that he weren't so obvious about being able to turn his interest in her on and off like a water tap. This current state of affairs couldn't be expected to last much longer anyway; Peter was bound to toy with her some evening when Ilse was otherwise engaged and he was in need of entertainment at a handy and unwary female's expense.

Gabi took her dishes to the sink and asked Frau Maurer for a postal bus schedule. She consulted the timetable and discovered that she could catch one of the bright yellow buses on the road from Heiligenschwendi and Goldiwil. The bus would drop her off in Thun within twenty minutes.

It was nice to know that she could get into town occasionally without having to rely on Peter for transport. After brushing her teeth and hair, Gabi got her camera and a sheaf of maps, which Peter had given her a few days after her arrival. She told Frau Maurer not to expect her for lunch; she would do her best to be back in time for dinner.

The bus wasn't crowded, and Gabi saw more of the scenery than she had during her travels with Peter, since she didn't have his overpowering male presence as a distraction. She left the bus at Thun's *Berntor,* or Bern Gate, and wandered on foot through the city center. It was quiet, as befitted a Sunday morning, although Gabi did see a reasonable number of children playing in the otherwise deserted side streets.

If only Peter were with me, she thought involuntarily when she walked past a sign that said *Keller-Theater,* or

"Cellar Theater." It would have been fun to have Peter suggest that they return some evening for a play or a cabaret performance. Gabi cut across a modern bridge to an island only a block wide and a few hundred yards long, which reminded her of pictures she had seen of the Île St-Louis in Paris. Trees were planted close together along the island's single street, and a careful exploration of the tiny islet revealed parks at both ends. The overall atmosphere was enchanting, perhaps even more so than on the Hauptgasse with its curious second-story sidewalks.

A narrow wooden bridge known as the "Old Sluice-Bridge" crossed the lower branch of the River Aare, joining the island's lakeside tip and the southern part of the mainland. Gabi found herself in a more modern section of town with a generous sprinkling of apartment blocks and commercial buildings. She consulted her map again and strolled to another park, which faced a short stretch of water that her map identified as the *Schiffs-kanal*. Two lake steamers were tied up, one on each side of the narrow canal; these were the boats Gabi had seen when arriving from Lucerne.

A sign told Gabi that the next boat left for Interlaken, at the other end of Lake Thun, at 1:30 P.M. The schedule indicated that the vessel would arrive at the landing stage of the Interlaken West railroad station two hours later.

Gabi was tempted to go on the boat. She had nothing better to do, and the weather probably wouldn't be this nice again till spring. She could always return from Interlaken West via train or bus and be back in time for supper.

On second thought, the idea of going on a lake excursion by herself seemed depressing. Most of the other people on the quay were with boyfriends, girlfriends, or families; taking the boat without a friend would be like going on a hayride without a companion of the opposite sex.

Gabi was about to leave the promenade when she noticed a young man looking at her curiously. He was handsome in a dandified way; he appeared to be the sort of young man who stayed fit in the interests of his appearance and not because he enjoyed physical exertion for its own sake. His blond hair was combed across a narrow head, and his eyes examined Gabi casually through a pair of stylish glasses. Gabi tried to pretend that she hadn't noticed his appraisal of her as she turned and began to walk away.

"Hallo!" a voice called out from behind her. "Fräulein!" Gabi hesitated, despite her wish to be left alone, and the British-accented voice continued, "You don't speak English by any chance, do you?"

Gabi looked around reluctantly and saw the young man walking toward her. Suddenly she realized that she had given herself away; now she would have to speak to him whether she cared to or not.

"You *do* speak English," he said when he stopped in front of Gabi and regarded her with a friendly gaze. "You look more American than English, though. Am I right?"

Gabi nodded. "Of Swiss descent," she added, for no other reason than to avoid being mistaken for an ordinary tourist.

"Kevin Fox is my name." His voice was boyish but not unpleasant. "I'm English, as you probably gathered from my accent if not from my inexcusably forward behavior. I hope you don't think I'm being fresh?"

"Not yet," Gabi said, and her succinct reply elicited a laugh from her accoster.

"I saw you looking at the boat schedule. Surely you aren't going to pass up the chance to see Lake Thun on a fine day like this?"

"I see it every day from my bedroom," Gabi said truthfully.

Kevin Fox looked intrigued by this but didn't comment. Instead, he insisted that she join him on the boat excursion.

Gabi was unwilling to say yes. After all, she didn't even know this young Englishman, although she had to admit that he looked fairly harmless. If he turned out to be an ill-mannered boor, he wouldn't be able to get very far with her on a lake steamer.

"Please," he cajoled. "I speak very little German, and there's no fun in going on an excursion like this alone."

"Exactly my thoughts," Gabi admitted, "but I insist on buying my own ticket."

"You do that, and I'll pop for tea."

It wasn't long until the two of them were comfortably seated in aluminum chairs with woven seats on the ship's lower deck just in front of the fantail. The Swiss flag with its bold white cross on a field of red fluttered in the breeze as the steamer moved out of the canal and onto the lake proper. The air currents weren't strong enough to make Gabi feel chilly, but they did keep her from becoming overly warm in the brilliant sunshine. She quickly put on sunglasses to tame the reflections off the blue water.

After insisting that they use first names, Kevin Fox gave Gabi a quick rundown on himself. "I live in London with my mother, which sounds terribly suspicious nowadays, but makes perfect sense when one considers that she has a ten-room flat and no one to share it with but her cook and maid. She also has a holiday flat here in Thun. That's where I'm staying, of course. It makes a pleasant change from the weather we've been having in England."

"And what do you do in London?" Gabi asked with the frankness of one who had been raised in the American Midwest.

"Not much, I'm afraid. I collect old books and write poetry for literary magazines, which are read by no one but their contributors. Fortunately, my father left a trust fund that makes it unnecessary for me to learn any sort of useful trade. I'm quite worthless by most people's standards, but at least I do maintain the British upper-class tradition of the gifted dilettante."

Gabi laughed. "You're so honest about yourself!"

"Why shouldn't I be honest? We English have a habit of cultivating eccentricity. I have nothing to be ashamed of." Kevin changed the subject by asking what Gabi was doing in Thun.

"I'm private secretary to an author," she replied.

"Is your writer a 'he' or a 'she'?" Kevin asked.

"A 'he.' I don't know if you've heard of him; his name may not be a household word in England. His name is Peter Imhof."

Kevin did a double take. "What an absolutely dreadful coincidence!"

"Don't tell me you know him?" Gabi asked with surprise.

"All too well," Kevin answered dryly. "But let's not talk about Peter Imhof. This is our afternoon; men like your employer shouldn't be allowed to intrude on it."

Kevin's attitude toward Peter made Gabi uncomfortable. She wondered if there were some terrible secret about Peter that she ought to know. "I wish you'd tell me what's so awful about him," she said.

Kevin shook his head. "Not now. Some other time."

"But—"

"Don't you love that view?" Kevin asked, waving a hand toward the shoreline as he abruptly changed the subject again. "In a little while we'll see the mountain near Spiez called the Niesen. It's an almost perfect pyramid. One can take a funicular up the Niesen, although I'm not sure if it's still running at this time of year."

Gabi gave up her attempt to squeeze more information about Peter out of Kevin. She would have to try again later. In the meantime she allowed herself to enjoy the boat trip, which wouldn't be over until half-past three, since the vessel zigzagged from one shore to the other on its trip to the lake's far end. There were to be twelve stops in all between Thun and Interlaken West, most of them in tiny villages.

Since it was the off-season, the boat wasn't at all crowded. Gabi and Peter were able to explore the vessel and spend some time in the lounge. Eventually Kevin insisted on taking Gabi into the buffet for a cup of tea or hot chocolate. "Did you have lunch? I believe they serve light meals," he offered.

Gabi settled for coffee and a pastry while Kevin ordered tea. It didn't take long for Gabi to decide that Kevin was a pleasant companion, far more so than Peter in many ways. He was witty at his own expense rather than Gabi's; he exuded a cheerful sort of charm that put her at her ease instead of making her feel like an awkward girl who was just out of junior high. Of course, he also seemed to have rather less depth than Peter. Gabi compared the two in her mind and found that Kevin came off second-best even if he was delightful company.

They reached Interlaken West in mid-afternoon. Kevin suggested that they go back by bus when he learned that Gabi had previously ridden the train from Interlaken to Thun via Spiez. "The buses run along the northern shore, so you'll see the lake from a different perspective."

The trip home involved a diesel bus to a village called Beatenbucht, where they switched to an electric trolleybus for the remainder of the ride. The whole journey took about an hour. They chatted idly on the way, and Gabi was still enjoying herself when they reached the Thun *busbahnhof* a little after five o'clock.

"May I ask you to dinner?" Kevin asked hopefully when they had alighted from the bus.

Gabi had to decline the invitation. "Frau Maurer is expecting me for supper," she explained.

"Ah, yes. The notorious Mr. Imhof's housekeeper. So be it; I'll drive you home." Kevin ignored Gabi's protests that she could wait for a postal bus. He took her by the elbow and guided her to a small and rather flashy-looking Japanese sports car, which was parked by the railroad station.

"I wish you'd tell me more about Peter," Gabi said when they were speeding along the road that led out of Thun.

"What is there to say? He's handsome, personable, and no doubt a brilliant writer in his field." Kevin smiled without conviction. "As a poet, I'm not terribly partial to novelists. Especially successful ones who steal my girls away."

Gabi stared at him. "What do you mean?"

"Are you sure you want to know?" Kevin asked, taking his eyes off the road just long enough to return her look. When she nodded, he continued: "All right. I met your employer's cousin Ilse at the casino in Thun last year. We were getting along famously—and still would be, if it hadn't been for your macho Herr Imhof. Apparently the two of them hit it off again after being separated for nearly four years. I believe the reunion took place at their uncle's funeral. In the past few weeks, since your boss moved into his late uncle's chalet . . . Well, I probably don't have to tell you, do I?"

"I really haven't been paying much attention to Peter's personal life," Gabi lied in what she feared was an unconvincing tone.

"If you ask me, it's the money," Kevin went on. "At any rate, Ilse has been drifting away from me at an alarming speed, much like galaxies in our ever-expanding universe. Perhaps you'd like to step into a starring role yourself, the newly vacant one of prospective fiancée." Kevin made this suggestion in a jocular tone, but there was an underlying hint of seriousness that left Gabi ill at ease. He continued almost self-mockingly: "Don't forget, I have a private income to make up for my lack of exploitable talents. And my mother tells me I'm really quite eligible, despite a tendency to talk too much."

Gabi laughed at this, unable to feel uncomfortable for long around this friendly young man who had such a harmless way of making her feel desirable. "I'll think about it," she promised without really meaning it.

Kevin eyed her shrewdly. "You aren't stuck on this Imhof fellow, are you?"

"Heaven forbid," said Gabi, but she knew as she spoke the words that her tone was too fervent.

Fortunately for Gabi's peace of mind, Kevin was too gentlemanly or too clever to acknowledge her blunder. He didn't say anything more about Peter. When they reached the chalet, he got out of the car and went around to help her with the door.

"Thanks for the lovely afternoon," Gabi said sincerely, reaching out for what she hoped would be nothing more intimate than a handshake.

Kevin gave a short laugh. "You didn't really think I'd settle for anything so mild as the chance to clasp your lovely fingers, did you?" When Gabi looked at him with alarm, he took her hand and kissed it like an Austrian nobleman. "There. My mother would call that my 'stamp of approval.' Here's hoping it will lead to bigger and better things."

Before Gabi could think of a reply, Kevin was back in the car and firing the ignition. *"Au revoir,"* he called while backing out of the driveway.

Gabi waved and mouthed a silent good-bye. Though she was relieved that he hadn't tried to kiss anything but her hand, she was almost sorry to see him go. Kevin was on his way to becoming the closest thing she had to a friend in Switzerland.

6

~~~~~~~~~~~~~~~~

Dinner was a tasty meal consisting of a Swiss beef stew with heavy white peasant bread and a fruit compote for dessert. The only thing wrong with it was the fact that Gabi had to eat it alone. She doubted if she would ever get used to dining by herself at the long oak table while Frau Maurer ate separately in the kitchen. Now and then she wondered if this were Frau Maurer's way of saying that she wasn't welcome in Peter's chalet. Probably not, Gabi decided; Frau Maurer was friendly enough in her reserved Swiss way, and she had shown approval along with her surprise when Gabi had insisted on making her own bed the morning after her arrival.

Gabi was listening to a record of Italian harpsichord music when the door from the foyer opened and Peter walked in with Winifred lumbering happily behind. He had dumped his bags in the hall and was now removing his trench coat, which he threw on a nearby chair on his way to the drinks cabinet.

"Enjoying yourself?" he asked in lieu of a greeting.

Gabi wasn't sure how to take the question. "In case

you've forgotten, you once said it was all right for me to use the stereo as long as I remembered to wipe the needle with alcohol after each playing."

"Now you're trying to embarrass me with my own Swiss thoroughness." A faint smile played across Peter's lips as he splashed a few ounces of rainwater Madeira into a snifter. He proffered the bottle. "Care for a drink?"

"No, thanks," Gabi said with a firm shake of her head.

"Perhaps you'd like some of that peppermint schnapps? It had a marvelous effect on you last time. As I recall, it unleashed impulses that you seemed unwilling to admit you'd ever felt before."

"I *hadn't* felt them before," Gabi said stiffly.

Peter gave her an odd look but didn't answer. Instead, he murmured the compulsory *"Prost!"* and raised his glass to her before downing its contents in one gulp.

"I gather that you had an exhausting trip," Gabi said as a picture of Ilse flashed across her mind.

"Not exhausting. Merely tiring. I always stay up too late at these literary affairs and drink too much wine with my contemporaries. Not enough to get drunk, mind you, but enough to affect my energy reserves the next day."

"Just what did you do in Zurich?" Gabi asked, wondering if Peter would make reference to his voluptuous second cousin.

"About what you'd expect. Committee meetings are the same the world over: a great deal of talk and little action. Some people enjoy that sort of thing; I'm not one of them."

"Then why take part?" Gabi asked while noting the lines of tiredness in his face and the shadows under his eyes.

"Duty, I suppose. Switzerland isn't a big country. I've

been away for four years, and I feel I should do my part in supporting the local writers' establishment now that I'm home. If my colleagues and I don't remind the outside world of our Swissness, we run the risk of being taken for Germans, Frenchmen, and Italians. Remember, Switzerland has only about six million people, compared to ten times that number in West Germany alone." He dashed another ounce of Madeira into his glass and sipped it while regarding Gabi speculatively, as if he were trying to reach some sort of conclusion about her.

"How did you return from Zurich?" Gabi asked to keep the conversation going.

"A train straight through to Bern. I transferred there for Thun; there was only a ten-minute wait."

"That isn't much time for changing trains," Gabi remarked.

Peter seemed amused by her cautious attitude. "The Swiss railroad timetable considers a transfer possible if there are two minutes between trains, unless the individual schedule says otherwise. One hardly ever fails to make a connection. I suppose that says something about our national compulsion for orderliness."

"Don't forget the compulsion for cleanliness, too," Gabi said lightly. "When I was on the train from Lucerne, I saw a streetsweeping machine cleaning a road out in the countryside."

Peter disposed of his empty glass and took a seat in one of the leather-upholstered armchairs while Winifred settled onto the rug at his feet. Gabi felt a wave of affection for this enigmatic man. He had left her; now he had returned. Granted, this was his house. He had come back to the chalet, not to her. Yet she couldn't help feeling somewhat like the wife who waits by the fireside for her man to return from a business trip. Her attitude would probably be altogether different tomorrow, when Peter was likely to be in one of his irritable moods because a scene wasn't going right in his novel or because he was afraid he might overstep his self-imposed moral bounds with her. But tonight was tonight. It was unfortunate that they couldn't enjoy more evenings like this together.

Peter made idle chat about Zurich, related a few lively anecdotes about his literary colleagues, and said nothing at all to suggest that he'd had female company during his weekend away from the chalet. He seemed too distracted to ask Gabi about her own weekend, and she didn't want to interrupt his reminiscences with an account of her activities. It was nice just to look at Peter and listen to him talk quietly in his deep, soothing voice. All I need is some knitting or crocheting to keep my hands busy, Gabi told herself with an inward smile. That way, the domestic mood would be nearly complete.

Peter's manner the next day was crisp without being unfriendly. He had beaten Gabi to the breakfast table but lingered over his coffee so they could chat while she had her own *milchkaffee* and rolls. Gabi decided to save her description of the steamer trip until later; she didn't want to hold up their morning's work.

She was taking dictation at a breakneck pace by nine o'clock. Peter's muse must have been working overtime, because he didn't finish reciting his descriptions and dialogue until shortly after noon. Gabi was exhausted when he called a halt and suggested that they go downstairs to lunch.

"I hope I wasn't going too fast for you this morning," Peter said while they waited for Frau Maurer to bring in their soup and pickled salad.

"Not really. My speed seems to be picking up a lot. I'm sure I must be taking down a hundred and fifty words a minute by now. I certainly got enough practice today."

Peter bit into a breadstick and looked at Gabi thoughtfully. "You weren't too bored this past weekend, were you?" he asked when he had finished chewing.

"Not at all," Gabi lied. "I enjoyed the peace and quiet."

Peter's lips twitched in a brief and not altogether amused smile. "Am I so hard to get along with when I'm here?"

"Well, you must admit that we rarely agree on anything," she said. "I only meant that it was nice to have enough time to get to know the area better on my own."

"And what part of the area did you get to know?"

Gabi hesitated, unwilling to say anything that might reveal her visit to Ilse's chalet. "Oh, I did some exploring on Saturday," she answered vaguely.

Peter nodded, but he was studying Gabi with slightly narrowed eyes, as if he knew she was trying to hide something from him.

"On Sunday I took the postal bus into Thun," Gabi said before he could demand a more detailed account of her walk.

"I could always get you a moped or a scooter," he suggested. "It would save you from worrying about the bus schedule on days when the weather is decent."

"Really, I'm perfectly happy taking the bus. It's nice that they have such frequent buses scheduled out here. I wouldn't have expected it, considering how small the villages are."

Peter leaned back while Frau Maurer placed a steaming bowl of cabbage-and-rice soup in front of him. "There's hardly a place in Switzerland that doesn't have some kind of bus or train service. Even a little *dörfli* at the top of a cliff with no road or rail access will generally be served by an aerial cable car. Switzerland is one of the few nations on earth where one can live just about anywhere and have reasonably good access to public transportation."

Gabi tasted her soup, found that it was too hot, and put her spoon down while waiting for the soup to cool.

"What did you do in Thun?" Peter asked casually.

"I walked around. And then . . ." For some reason she was nervous about telling him of the boat trip. Was it because she had been with Kevin the whole time? "I took a lake steamer to Interlaken," she said at last.

"Alone?"

Gabi flushed, and the heat in her cheeks told her that she had given away her secret.

"Don't tell me you've already found a boyfriend," Peter said in a sardonic tone.

"Not exactly." She explained how she had been ready to skip the boat trip when a young man spoke to her in English and insisted that she go along with him.

"And do you always do what men insist?" Peter asked dryly.

Gabi glared at him, her embarrassment giving way to anger. "You weren't there. It was all perfectly innocent. If you hadn't gone to Zurich—"

"Now you're saying I should have stayed home to

entertain you, is that it?" he said with an irritating disregard for logic.

"I didn't say that. But I *do* think I have the right to do a little sightseeing on my own if I'm not needed here at the chalet."

Peter's expression softened a little, but there was still a coolness in his gaze. "I wouldn't have thought you were the type to pick up strange men."

"I didn't pick anyone up. And Kevin didn't pick me up. We—"

"Kevin?" Peter interrupted sharply.

Gabi lowered her gaze to her soup bowl. Why on earth had she let his name slip out?

"Not Kevin Fox?" Peter continued impatiently.

Gabi nodded, unable to speak.

"He's nothing but a layabout. Surely you can find better pickings than Kevin Fox," Peter said with heavy sarcasm.

"Kevin is a friend, that's all." Gabi knew she sounded defensive, and the knowledge made her angry with herself. "I really don't think that it's any of your business anyway."

"You've met Fox once, and you already call him a friend? *Du lieber Himmel!* You do work fast."

Gabi's fury now directed itself at Peter. "Will you stop talking to me like that?"

"Someone has to look out for your interests," Peter said more calmly. "Since you no longer have parents to give you the guidance you so obviously require, I find myself forced into the role of counselor and guardian."

"You're my employer, nothing else," Gabi retorted.

"Nothing else?" His tone was now one of amusement.

"Nothing else," Gabi repeated, knowing it was a lie but not caring. Is my attraction to him that obvious? she asked herself with a trace of frustration. Will he always be able to read me like an open book?

Gabi had hoped to be free of Peter's disconcerting presence after lunch, but this afternoon he went upstairs with her to pencil-edit the previous Friday's typescript while she transcribed his latest material. She didn't know why he was doing it, unless it was a conscious ploy to make her ill at ease.

Having Peter in the library caused Gabi to make more errors than usual, but Peter at least had the decency not to comment on her frequent pauses for corrections. It was after three o'clock when she finished typing up the new sections of manuscript.

Gabi was about to go downstairs to her room when Peter surprised her by asking if she cared to join him on a walk. "We'll have Winifred along as chaperone," he added with a smile.

It was hard to tell if he really wanted her to join him or if he were merely being polite. Gabi decided that he must be trying to compensate for his unkindness at lunch. "I'd love to," she replied.

Soon they were in the Porsche with Winifred occupying the space behind the bucket seats. Peter drove uphill toward Heiligenschwendi until he reached a spot where they could leave the car. From there, a marked footpath led upward to the rocky crest of the ridge.

The woods were cool but pleasant; every so often Peter and Gabi would cross a clearing that felt surprisingly warm in the afternoon sun. Gabi enjoyed listening to

Peter's comments on the local topography and vegetation. It was nice to be friendly with him again; Gabi always felt vaguely disappointed when tension existed between them.

After a while they reached a secluded clearing where Peter suggested that they pause for a rest. To Gabi's surprise, he took a nylon ground cloth from his rucksack and spread it out on the soft grass. "Make yourself comfortable," he said while removing a canteen and several other items from the canvas pack.

Winifred flopped down nearby and seemed grateful for the bowl of water that Peter poured out. He finished serving Winifred and took a swig from his canteen. "Thirsty?" he asked, proffering the flask to Gabi.

Gabi nodded. Her pulse accelerated as she took the water bottle from Peter; she credited this to the altitude and the exertion. It can't have anything to do with my sharing Peter's water flask, she told herself. Still, an indefinable excitement flooded her senses when she put the bottle's metal opening to her lips and tasted the water that had been warmed inside the rucksack by Peter's body heat. Normally Gabi hated to share bottles or cups with other people, but somehow this occasion was different. Peter wasn't just anyone. He was . . . well, he was Peter. The knowledge that she had put him in a special category startled her, and she choked as a drop of water got caught in her windpipe.

Peter leaned forward and took the flask from her hands. "Are you all right? Do you want me to pat you on the back? Or should I administer the kiss of life?" His tone was amused yet sympathetic at the same time.

"I don't think that will be necessary," Gabi answered

with a forced air of indifference that failed to hide her momentary discomposure.

"The kiss of peace, then, in hopes of calling a ceasefire in this war of wills that exists between us." Peter didn't give Gabi time to think of a rejoinder; he was already easing her down onto the ground cloth, his upper torso moving over her to blot out the afternoon sun. Gabi opened her mouth to protest and was met with a kiss that pressed her head against the earth. She tried to wriggle out of Peter's embrace but was held fast by the weight of his chest and by his elbows, which prevented any sideways movement of her body. Her immobility left her angry and frustrated; and then her resentment was washed away in the flood of sweet desire that was unleashed by his deep, penetrating kiss.

The exertions of the hike had left both of them warm. Gabi now sensed the heat of Peter's body through her layers of clothing. As he released her mouth to murmur something—a challenge? an endearment?—Gabi twisted, trying to break free of the arms that encircled her writhing body.

Peter shifted against her full length, smothering her resistance and Gabi felt his tongue taking possession of her, as he ravished her with a kiss such as she had never imagined in her wildest fantasies. Her trepidation gave way to joy: the joy of a kiss that was almost cosmic in its intensity, the rapture of an embrace that pushed all conscious thought aside, as Gabi was overwhelmed by the urgency of her need for Peter.

Gabi returned his probing kiss until Peter gently disengaged himself from her trembling body and let his fingers stray to the buttons of her sweater. She felt her heart thumping madly and a stirring of anticipation when Peter began to unbutton her plaid flannel shirt.

"A woman has no business dressing like a lumber-jack," Peter mumbled, pushing the shirt's scratchy lapels out of the way and applying a thumb and index finger to the hook of Gabi's front-fastening bra.

Gabi suppressed a gasp when the brassiere's lacy cups fell away. She felt the tingling points of her breasts swell into throbbing proof of her eagerness as they were exposed to the sunshine and to Peter's hungry gaze. Peter now lowered his lips to kiss her rosy nipples one at a time. Gabi closed her eyes. The sweet yet fiery surge of pleasure inspired by his kisses was tainted by the knowledge that she was being used. If he were doing this because he truly felt something for her . . . but no; he was punishing her, taking his revenge by stripping her of her clothes and her inhibitions. Nonetheless, an almost unbearable eagerness gripped her, sweeping away her reservations as Peter's fingers, brushing her bare stomach, toyed seductively with the metal button at the waistband of her jeans.

Gabi was arching her body against Peter's in helpless surrender when Winifred unexpectedly jumped up from the grass and let out a warning bark. Peter's hand froze, stopping just short of the place where Gabi was already opening herself to him like a blossoming flower.

"Damn." He followed this with a muffled oath in Swiss-German dialect before rising to his feet and turning away so that Gabi couldn't see his facial expression or the proof of his need for her. "You'd better get dressed," she heard him say in a voice that somehow had become almost brusque only seconds after he had shown himself ready, through his actions, to lead her across exciting new frontiers of intimacy.

Gabi scrambled to her knees and buttoned the sweater without bothering to fasten her shirt or bra. "What is it?" she asked in a voice that sounded too weak and high-pitched to be her own.

"Winifred must hear someone coming."

A crunch of twigs announced the arrival of the herdsman whom Gabi credited, not altogether gratefully, with the preservation of her self-respect. The shepherd was a middle-aged peasant with a floppy hat and a bushy salt-and-pepper beard that wouldn't have looked out of place in a western movie. He was smoking an upside-down pipe whose bowl was covered with a perforated metal lid. A small flock of young goats scampered at his heels.

"*Gruezi,*" the man said with a shrewd glance in Gabi's direction.

Gabi blushed crimson and murmured an embarrassed "gruezi" of her own. Peter's greeting was friendly enough in an offhand way; he showed no signs of the irritation he must have felt at the herdsman's awkwardly timed intrusion.

Soon the flock of goats and their master were beyond the clearing. Gabi looked at Peter expectantly, thinking that he would carry on from where they had left off. But the fire had gone out of his need for her, and he appeared to be in control of himself when he bent down and folded the nylon ground cloth. "It's late," he said in an expressionless tone. "We'd better head back.

Gabi nodded dully. Did he find her so unappealing that he could turn his desire on and off at will? Burning with embarrassment, she faced the other way and unbuttoned her sweater so she could fasten her bra and shirt. She half-expected, half-hoped that Peter would come up from behind and insist on helping. But he didn't, and he wasn't even looking her way when she finished arranging her clothes and turned around again. Instead, he was squatting next to Winifred and rubbing her ears affectionately.

I need a hot bath, Gabi told herself unhappily after she had locked the door of the bathroom and hung her robe on the hook. She ran water in the tub while searching through the assortment of bath salts on a conveniently placed shelf until she found a floral-scented bubble bath that she hadn't tried before.

It felt good to slide down into the steaming water and let the soap bubbles tickle her nose. Gabi's limbs were aching from the long uphill hike, and she felt a deeper ache that was more difficult to explain. She decided that the latter wasn't an ache so much as it was an unfamiliar tension, a feeling that something had been started and not quite finished. The knowledge of what her mind was half-consciously dwelling on made Gabi grow warm and stretch languorously in the hot, scented water.

A moment later she was rebuking herself for her self-indulgent thoughts. She had come perilously close to losing her self-respect this afternoon. If he had succeeded in carrying out his intentions. . . . Gabi shuddered and changed position restlessly in the tub. I couldn't have gone on working for him if he had made love to me, she told herself with a forcefulness that she normally reserved for her disagreements with Peter. Fortunately, Peter usually remembered the danger in going too far with her;

hence his early warning on the balcony that they should avoid compromising situations in the future.

Gabi reached for the hand shower attachment and began to wash her hair. The hike hadn't made her especially sweaty, but she nevertheless felt a compulsion to get really clean. It was partly her fault that Peter had nearly taken advantage of her. He might have been content with a kiss if she hadn't responded so fervently to his caresses.

Gabi finished rinsing her hair and stood up in the tub, sluicing off the fragrant bath bubbles with the hand shower while the bathwater drained away at her feet. She then wrapped herself in one of the chalet's huge towels and used a smaller one to dry her hair. Gabi felt better now that she had bathed. Her tension had been shed with the soapsuds. Peter could be as patronizing as he wished at dinner; Gabi wouldn't care. Her mother had once said that the best way to deal with insults was to ignore them. No doubt the same rule could be applied to Peter's dry smiles and double entendres.

Peter was freshly showered and dressed in a casual but elegantly tailored suit of Harris tweed when Gabi went into the living room a short while later. He took one look at her clinging magenta dress and raised his aperitif glass in a toast. "Ilse will be beside herself when she sees you," he said good-humoredly.

Gabi stiffened. "Ilse?" she echoed as calmly as she could.

"She's coming to dinner. She called up a while ago to say that she was lonesome, and fortunately Frau Maurer was preparing the kind of dinner that can be stretched to feed a guest."

Gabi turned and folded her arms so Peter wouldn't see that her hands were clenched into fists. How could he be so cruel? Didn't he realize how much pain he caused by nearly seducing her, then using Ilse to remind her that he was already deeply involved with another woman? Why couldn't he simply leave her alone and be content with Ilse? Ilse was certainly sexy enough. Gabi found it hard to believe that the other girl's sophistication didn't carry over into bed.

"Would you like an aperitif?" Peter's voice came from a point near her right ear as he laid a hand on her shoulder from behind.

Gabi jerked from his grasp. If only he would stop touching her! Why couldn't he be like other Swiss males and limit himself to an occasional jerky handshake?

"I have an excellent Manzanilla you might want to try," Peter said with a dryness that matched that of the wine he offered her.

"A Coke, please."

"I beg your pardon?" His tone implied disbelief.

"Any kind of soft drink, then. Or some of that bottled grape juice. I don't want anything alcoholic."

Peter went to the liquor cabinet while Gabi's eyes followed him. He opened the lower door, which conceal-ed a small refrigerator. She watched him take out a bottle of Coke, uncap it, and pour it with great ceremony into an enormous snifter. Gabi flushed with irritation when he handed her the glass. She suspected he had picked the snifter to make her feel conspicuous with her soft drink when Ilse arrived.

"You're sure you wouldn't like a little rum in that? Or maybe a different drink altogether?" Peter's eyes twinkled with amusement. "Ilse seems to bring out the worst in you. You might be better off with a good dose of alcohol to help you relax."

"I am relaxed," Gabi declared. "Or at least I *was* relaxed when I came downstairs."

Ignoring the implications in her tone, Peter's eyes now rested on her breasts. "That's a charming dress."

"Thank you." Gabi accepted the compliment grudgingly.

"I'm sorry about Ilse. Not sorry that I invited her, but that you find her so difficult to get along with. She is my cousin, and she enjoys being in this house because she came here often during her childhood. One also mustn't forget that she took care of Uncle Jakob here during the final months of his life."

Gabi merely shrugged, unwilling to display her skepticism openly. She told herself that Peter couldn't possibly be so obtuse as to think that nostalgia was what prompted Ilse's visits to the chalet. Suddenly Gabi remembered what Kevin had said: that Ilse was eager to marry Peter because of the large amount of money he had inherited. Was that true? If so, did Peter have any inkling of Ilse's motives, or was he too distracted by her beauty and sophistication to give a thought to the nature of her interest in him?

Gabi made a quick decision. "If you don't mind, I'll eat in my room tonight," she told Peter.

His eyebrows rose a notch. "But I do mind, *Liebchen.*"

"Don't be silly. I'm sure the two of you would be much happier without me." A trace of petulance had entered Gabi's voice.

"If you're offended by what you regard as silliness, I

suggest that you take a moment to analyze your own behavior," Peter said reasonably. "You can't refuse to be civil to other people just because you don't like them."

"I never said I didn't like Ilse. I just said—" Gabi stopped, unable to recall what things she might have said about the other woman.

"You don't need to say it, Gabi. You look at Ilse with all the affection of a museum curator who's forced to make cocktail party chatter with a known art thief. It's no wonder that she treats you badly."

Gabi took a deep breath. At least he admitted that Ilse treated her badly! Perhaps he would eventually see that the ill feeling between herself and Ilse had been started by Ilse and not the other way around.

"It isn't worth arguing over," Gabi heard herself saying with a haughty air. "I'll eat upstairs and keep out of your way. Ilse will be grateful."

Peter sighed. "Please dine with us," he persisted. "I can't let you go into hiding just because my cousin is here. I'd like you to become more comfortable with her. Try and get used to the idea of having her around."

Gabi's heart was seized by a stab of pain. Now, what on earth did he mean by that? Was this the first formal hint that he and Ilse were already discussing marriage?

She turned and walked to the window, where she stared unseeingly at the lake in the distance. Why did I ever come here? she asked herself. The whole thing had been a mistake; she should have known back in Chicago that working for this attractive and arrogantly seductive man was bound to end in heartbreak, or at least in disappointment.

Peter was standing directly behind her now. Gabi didn't object when he took her snifter and placed it on a nearby table. Instead, she spoke in a voice that threatened to choke up at any moment: "If you aren't sure you want me to stay the six months we originally agreed upon—"

"Don't be ridiculous. We have an agreement, and I expect you to stick by it."

"You could always get Ilse to fill in after I left, until you could find someone else."

Peter dismissed this suggestion with a smile that Gabi found infuriating. "Ilse can't take shorthand, nor does she have your command of English. Besides, she has other interests besides secretarial work."

"And you think I don't?" Gabi stepped away from Peter, reeling at the insult. She could well imagine what Ilse's "other interests" were: Peter, money, or a combination of both.

"I'm not going to eat dinner with you," Gabi said with a stubbornness born of pride. She knew better than to argue any further about leaving Switzerland; Peter's mind obviously was made up on that point.

"You'll join us for dinner, or you'll go without," Peter warned, wagging his finger at her.

"You're treating me like a recalcitrant child!"

"If you insist on behaving like a child, how can you object to my treating you like one?" Peter replied calmly.

Infuriated by his maddening self-assurance, Gabi stepped back and aimed the flat of her hand at Peter's cheek. The attempt to defend her injured pride was useless; strong fingers grasped her wrist when her palm was still a foot away from its target. Gabi tried to jerk her hand free and felt herself being spun around so that Peter's arms could encircle her rib cage from behind.

"I won't fight with you," Peter murmured softly. "But

maybe I can subdue you in a more pleasant way instead." His mouth dropped to the side of her neck, kissing her with a delicacy that was as pleasurable as it was unexpected. Gabi opened her mouth in surprise and felt her knees growing weak in spite of Peter's high-handed manner. His hands began to caress her breasts through the jersey dress, seeking the responsive tips and stroking them until Gabi could no longer pretend to be indifferent to his touch. Her head fell backward onto his shoulder. She tilted her face upward and closed her eyes for the inevitable kiss.

Peter's lips grazed hers teasingly at first, then settled against her mouth. He ran his tongue intimately over her lips until she finally opened her mouth, allowing him to explore the warm softness within. There was no denying her sudden adventurousness or the sensations that were spreading like wildfire through her awakening body. Gabi felt Peter's tongue return her kiss with an intensity that was echoed in the hardness of his body against the feminine softness of her own. His embrace tightened; his mouth moved from her lips to her neck again, where he nibbled gently at the curves of her throat until she thought she would explode from the sweet yet exquisite need that welled up inside her.

Suddenly Gabi heard the click of a door and the noise of a woman's heels coming to a stop just short of the living room carpet. Her eyes flew open. Gabi's shocked gaze was met by a look of unconcealed hatred from Ilse Delacroix, who stood ten feet away in a dress as black as the mood that revealed itself in her expression.

"I seem to be interrupting something," Ilse said coldly.

Gabi felt Peter's arms release themselves from her body. Her cheeks were hot with embarrassment as she broke away from him and turned blindly toward the staircase.

She was halfway to the landing when she was intercepted by Peter, who smoothly passed her the snifter of soft drink and steered her back toward the couch in the living room. "Please, Gabi. There's no need to rush off in such a hurry," he said quietly.

Ice had flashed into steam where Ilse was concerned. She glared first at Gabi, then turned to Peter. "Miss Studer was perhaps intending to retire to her room for the evening," she hissed at him.

Peter's equanimity wasn't disturbed in the least by Ilse's blatant show of jealousy. "On the contrary—I believe she was rather enjoying herself down here." The look that he aimed at Gabi was almost challenging, as though he were daring her to fight Ilse for his affections. Gabi's knees felt wobbly. For some reason Peter had singled her out to play the victim's role in an event no less cruel than a dogfight or cockfight.

"Your sense of humor is extremely distasteful at times, Peter," Ilse said with greater control than she had displayed a moment earlier. Her voice carried a hint of sarcasm when she added: "Still, you never did like being taked for granted, did you?"

Peter's eyes narrowed slightly, but he didn't respond verbally to the jibe. He merely rested a hand at the small of Gabi's back, where the tips of his fingers imprinted a fiery message of possession on Gabi's sensitive spine.

Frau Maurer appeared in the kitchen doorway to announce that dinner would be served in fifteen minutes. "In that case," said Peter, "I'd better get you a glass of wine, Ilse." He sounded oddly pleased with himself, and Gabi realized, in a sudden flash of understanding, that

Peter must be using her to make his cousin jealous. Why else would he have prevented her from going upstairs and made her return to the living room? For what other reason would he impose her presence on the elegant, mercenary young woman who seemed destined to become his wife?

7

~~~~~~~~~~~~~~~~~~~~~

The next week was a period of nearly unbearable tension for Gabi. Though Peter made no direct reference to what had happened in the mountain clearing and in the chalet, he showed distinct signs of being on edge from having to restrain his impulses when he was near her. It was obvious to Gabi that he wasn't the kind of man to take unfinished business lightly, yet at the same time he continued to give her the impression, through his words and actions, that he didn't intend to lose a competent secretary by prematurely venting his physical frustrations in a way that might make a working relationship intolerable.

Of course, there could be other motives for Peter's failure to resume his twice-interrupted lovemaking. Maybe he was thinking of firing her. If that should be the case, he would want to keep the situation between them under control until he could find a replacement. Or perhaps Ilse had laid down the law by demanding that Peter keep his hands off Gabi if he didn't want their unannounced betrothal to end before it had officially begun.

commitment." Peter looked at Gabi with narrowed eyes that revealed more than a hint of suspicion.

Gabi took her hands from the tabletop and rested them in her lap so Peter wouldn't notice that they had begun to tremble. "In other words, you believe romantic love is never anything more than self-deception and wishful thinking?"

"I didn't say that." Peter ran a hand through his thick curly hair, then turned his head so that Gabi couldn't see his expression as he stared through the plate glass window at the shoppers on the Hauptgasse. "Statistical probability enters into it, of course. It's like the old story about supplying typewriters to a roomful of monkeys. If they were all permitted to tap at the keys for a lifetime, it's quite likely that one of them might eventually come up with a complete sentence. The same odds can result in a very satisfying case of lasting romantic love. But few people are so lucky. For most of us, love is a fiction. We're fortunate if we end up with a spouse who is merely compatible."

"And what do you call 'compatible'?" Gabi asked in a voice that was devoid of all emotion.

"The ability to live together without fighting constantly, to accept each other's foibles and enjoy a modicum of erotic pleasure and emotional comfort with one's chosen companion."

"That isn't as easy as it sounds," Gabi said while her fingers slowly tore a paper napkin to shreds.

"No, it isn't. It was much simpler in the old days when a man learned his father's trade and a woman married in order to care for a husband and bear his children. No one expected a great deal out of life, and those who lived to a ripe old age without losing more than a child or two to illness considered themselves blessed by God."

Gabi forced herself to look directly at Peter. "Would you honestly be happy with that kind of life?"

"It has its merits," he replied cryptically.

Gabi wasn't satisfied with his answer. She tried unsuccessfully to keep the tension from her voice as she plunged ahead. "Let me put it another way. Would your cousin Ilse be happy with that kind of life?"

Peter made a disparaging gesture. "I daresay she'd be more than content with such a life if the incentives were great enough in terms of money, power, and prestige."

"And that doesn't bother you?" Gabi asked, horrified by his honesty.

"Why should it? Ilse is as entitled to her happiness as anyone else is." Peter was smiling, but his eyes had narrowed again in a way that suggested Gabi was now treading on delicate ground.

"I think your attitude is despicable!" Gabi cried. She threw the remnants of her paper napkin on the table and snatched up her purse. Two elderly ladies in a nearby booth stared at her with open disapproval of her behavior, but Gabi didn't even notice. She turned her back on Peter and marched from the bakery. Her gesture was in vain, of course; that became obvious as soon as she realized that Peter would only be waiting for her when she got back to the chalet on the postal bus. Still, Gabi wasn't about to ride home in the Porsche after listening to Peter endorse Ilse's mercenary behavior. Futile as her gesture might be, it was a gesture. And gestures—even futile ones—were at least more satisfying than listening to Peter spell out the nature of his relationship with Ilse in that infernally polite manner in which he had been torturing her for the past week.

Though it was already November, the weather in the Bernese Oberland wasn't quite as chilly as Chicago's was at this time of year. Only the frequent drizzle and occasional fog kept Gabi from working off her frustrations with daily hikes in the surrounding woods and meadows.

Gabi took advantage of one relatively sunny weekend by catching the trolleybus to Beatenbucht, halfway along the northern lake shore, and riding the cableway to Beatenberg. The latter village was spread across a long terrace on a mountain called the Niederhorn, some 1,640 feet above Lake Thun. There was an indoor swimming pool, which Gabi found quite pleasant; she also enjoyed the magnificent view of the entire Bernese Alpine range. She spent the afternoon there and decided to return in the winter tourist season when the chairlift to the Niederhorn's ridge would be running again.

On another occasion Gabi donned woolen knickers, knee socks, hiking boots, and a rainproof parka for a stroll through the bird sanctuary at Einigen near Thun. She would have liked to climb the Stockhorn, a dramatic-looking mountain whose 7,100-foot summit overlooked Thun, but a clerk in the city's tourist office suggested that it would be wiser to wait until the return of warm weather.

If she couldn't climb the Stockhorn, then she could at least visit the overlook in Thun and identify the many individual peaks in the Bernese alps with the diagram on the engraved viewing table. Gabi regretted having failed to take in the *Wocher Panorama*, a huge circular painting of Thun done in 1800, before it closed for the season in late October. She very much doubted if she would ever get to see it since the exhibit didn't open again till April. It no longer seemed likely that she would continue working for Peter once her obligatory six months were up.

There were so many sights to see in the area that Gabi hardly knew which to visit first. One day she rode the bus into Thun after supper and wandered along the lakeside promenade. It was a drizzly evening, but lights could be seen in the distance, and Gabi even thought she saw a train speeding along the southern shore of the lake. If only Peter had come with her! His presence would have made her feel romantic instead of melancholy. But he'd had other plans for the evening; no doubt he was off cavorting with Ilse. Gabi knew that Peter had to see Ilse frequently because of business matters involving their late uncle's estate, but there was nothing to keep him from combining business with pleasure.

Saturday came, and Gabi told Peter that she intended to go into Bern for the day. He looked at her for a moment and then shook his head. "Wait," he said.

"Wait for what? I've been here more than a month now, and I still haven't visited the city where I was born."

"I'd just as soon you waited until I can go with you," Peter told her.

"But why? Surely you don't think I'll get lost in Bern and never return to finish working on your novel?" she teased him.

"It isn't that. I simply think you'd enjoy Bern more if you had company—someone to show you the little sights along with the big ones. I'd take you in today, but unfortunately I have to deliver a lecture to a group of booksellers in Interlaken." He sounded sincere, and Gabi was pleased by his seemingly genuine desire to help her enjoy her first visit to Bern since leaving that city as an infant. After the tension that had existed between them lately, his thoughtfulness seemed out of character.

Gabi ended up doing her laundry and helping Frau Maurer with her mending chores. Frau Maurer wasn't one to throw away a sheet or napkin when it frayed. Instead, she got out her darning egg and needle and repaired the damage with the inbred thriftiness of the native Swiss. Gabi was relearning long-forgotten domestic skills under Frau Maurer's tutelage. The housekeeper seemed to approve of Gabi's interest, even if she was firm about not letting her pupil do more than a token share of the work.

Peter looked at Gabi with concern when he walked into the kitchen that afternoon and found her drinking a popular Swiss herb beverage with Frau Maurer.

"*Ricola?*" he asked, frowning. "What's the matter, do you have a sore throat?"

Gabi shook her head. "Frau Maurer asked if I'd ever tried it. When I said no, she insisted that I join her for a cup."

Peter examined the can of granulated beverage mix, which Frau Maurer had left on the countertop. "I haven't had any of this in years. What a list of ingredients! Linden flowers, elder, sage, horehound, peppermint, angelica root . . . and menthol. How could I have forgotten?" He smiled. "My mother used to insist that I drink this when I was ill. It was like drinking herb tea and cough medicine heated together and fortified with a heavy dose of sugar. Trust the Swiss to come up with something like this! We have to pay for our sweets with suffering."

"I'm not suffering," Gabi countered. "I like the way it tastes."

"It's just the thing if you have strep throat," Peter said dryly. "Or tonsillitis."

"Frau Maurer says it can be soothing anytime."

"And you feel in need of soothing?" Peter asked with lifted eyebrows.

Gabi avoided his eyes. "Well, it is a cold day."

"A cognac would do just as well if the cold is what's bothering you," Peter suggested.

"I don't like cognac."

"No, you prefer sweet drinks, don't you? Sugar to compensate for the tartness of your tongue."

"You're making fun of me," Gabi said with a flash of anger at what she took to be a patronizing tone.

"On the contrary. I'm appreciating you for what you are."

"And what am I?" Gabi asked doubtfully.

"A girl who's on the threshold of growing up. Someone balanced rather precariously between childhood and womanhood, between—"

"Oh, shut up!"

Peter's eyebrows rose another sixteenth of an inch before dropping back to their normal level. "Like a child, you're quick to anger and far too inclined to rudeness."

"I suppose you're going to add that Swiss children are never as rude as their American counterparts," Gabi said as her fingers gripped her teacup.

"Very seldom, anyway. They're raised in a stricter environment, one where rude behavior isn't tolerated to the degree that it may be in the country where you were raised. Violence may not be a Swiss characteristic, but that doesn't mean Swiss parents aren't willing to give a spanking when it's deserved." Peter's eyes bored into Gabi's, and there was a clear message to be read in his gaze. Mind your manners or else, he seemed to be telling her. His paternal attitude infuriated Gabi, but for once she kept her emotions in check as she quietly looked away from him and finished the cup of sweet mentholated beverage that soothed the throat if not the soul.

On the following Saturday, Gabi took the bus into Thun in order to shop for toiletries and to buy a small gift for a former co-worker back in Chicago who was having a baby soon. She emerged from a *drogerie* on the Hauptgasse to see a familiar vehicle pull up to the curb. The car's driver was Kevin Fox. Gabi had mixed feelings about seeing him; Kevin invariably made her think of Ilse, and thoughts of Ilse were the last thing she needed anytime. Still, Kevin already had caught her eye, so it was too late to make a discreet getaway.

"Join me for a pastry," he insisted when he had climbed out of the little sports car. "A *kremeschnitte*, perhaps. I'm in a *kremeschnitte* mood. How about you?"

"I hadn't thought of defining my mood in terms of pastries," Gabi said, unable to resist a smile. "Maybe a slice of Black Forest cake would be appropriate, though, for my black weekend mood."

"And is your mood always dismal on weekends?" Kevin asked as he slipped a hand under Gabi's elbow and guided her toward a café.

"No. I was only kidding," Gabi said defensively, not wanting him to know that he had made her think of Ilse.

"In that case, let's try *tartelettes aux marrons*. Chest-

127

nut tarts for a tart young woman who only occasionally needs Kevin to nod sympathetically while she gets her troubles off her chest."

Gabi laughed. She had no way of guessing Kevin's skills as a poet, but she had to admit that he loved puns.

They found a table in a café overlooking the Hauptgasse's second-story promenade. Kevin immediately apologized for not having telephoned since their last meeting. "I've been in England," he explained. "Mother had a birthday, and I had to go back to plan a surprise bash."

"Was she surprised?" Gabi asked politely.

"Not really. But it suits her vanity to have a party sprung on her instead of being asked to join in its planning. It's hard to be a convincing guest of honor when you're running the show yourself."

Gabi decided to try some traditional Bernese spice cookies, formed with wooden molds and decorated with white sugar bears. Kevin ordered a pair of napoleons, or *kremeschnitten*, in keeping with his professed mood, and they both asked the waitress for big cups of rich Swiss coffee.

"How long do you expect to stay in Thun this time?" Gabi asked while waiting for their coffee to be served.

"It all depends on how enchanting I find the company." Kevin's meaningful glance made it clear to whom the word "company" referred.

"What about Ilse?" asked Gabi.

"Let's not speak of the dead," he answered wryly. "Ilse is a lost cause. Too bad, really. Mother would have thought her a very suitable mate." Kevin cast a speculative glance in Gabi's direction. "Come to think of it, you have just as much to offer except money. And with taxes being what they are in England these days, what good is the extra income anyway? If I'm going to marry, I might as well do it for love as for cash."

Kevin's words were so cheerfully outrageous that Gabi couldn't take offense at his implication that he had never cared about anything but Ilse's money and was now willing to give his heart to Gabi, the one girl he really loved.

It was after five o'clock when they finished their coffee and pastries. Kevin suggested that .Gabi join him for a movie and supper afterwards. Gabi shook her head, saying that Frau Maurer and Peter were expecting her back for dinner at six o'clock.

"So?" argued Kevin. "Simply call your housekeeper and tell her you've run into a long-lost friend. Say it's an old chum who showed up unexpectedly on a bus tour, and that you're going to have dinner after exploring the souvenir shops together." He grinned, and Gabi reluctantly began looking for a pay phone.

She felt a little better about going out with Kevin once they were in the modern *kino*, which faced the inner branch of the River Aare. It was nice to see a film again, even if she would have enjoyed it more in Peter's company.

The movie was French with German subtitles. It was about a love triangle that involved a millionaire businessman, his wife, and his mistress. Gabi found herself identifying with the wife even though the mistress was more attractive. The wife was almost painfully naive, being concerned with her infant child and with maintaining a comfortable home for her husband. The mistress was the exact opposite: a calculating woman who was also sexy and beautiful. Gabi found herself becoming more and more depressed as the film wore on. She wasn't mollified by the rather ridiculous ending, which had the two women fighting over the husband until he marched both of them onto his private jet and flew them to the Middle East, where he took the mistress as a second wife, dressed both women in *djellabas* and veils, and ordered them to live happily ever after with him.

"Charming film, wasn't it?" Kevin said, as he and Gabi left the theater. "The French certainly have a way with bedroom comedy."

As the Swiss, or at least the Swiss-Americans, have a knack for bedroom tragedy, Gabi thought, without answering Kevin's remark about the movie.

Kevin suggested they have dinner at the Hotel Falken, a comfortable riverside establishment not far from the theater.

The Hotel Falken's dining room was fairly busy, considering that it had been several weeks since the official end of the tourist season. Gabi wasn't very hungry but made no objections when Kevin recommended that she try the *Bernerplatte,* a Bernese specialty consisting of pork and sausages served on a bed of sauerkraut with green beans. The portions turned out to be enormous; still, Gabi did a creditable job of cleaning her plate once her appetite had been stimulated by a few tentative nibbles.

Kevin carried the conversation throughout most of the meal. After a while Gabi managed to work things around to Peter and Ilse. "How much do you really know about their feelings for each other?" she asked with a casualness she didn't feel.

"I know only what must be clear to anyone who keeps his or her eyes open," Kevin said. "Ilse has checked out

Peter's bank account and decided that a rich Swiss is a better investment than a moderately well-off Englishman. One can't blame her, really; the pound sterling is frequently almost as tarnished as your dollar, whereas the Swiss franc is backed by more than enough gold to keep Ilse in expensive trinkets for the rest of her life."

After dinner, Kevin suggested that they go to a place called the Dancing-Bar Oasis. "It's about time I got to put my arms around you without risking a slap for bad behavior," he said with a meaningful wink.

Gabi shook her head. "I'm not much of one for dancing."

"Come to my flat, then. We can have a drink before I take you home. Don't be so suspicious," Kevin said with another of his disarming smiles. "You know how harmless I am. What would my mother say if I went and got arrested for molesting innocent young women?"

Kevin's gentle pleadings were hard to resist, especially since it was only nine o'clock and Gabi wasn't in the mood to go back to the chalet. "All right," she agreed, telling herself that Kevin wasn't likely to sweep her off her feet and into his bed.

The apartment took up four rooms in a three-story building on the outskirts of town. It was pleasant in a decorator-inspired sort of way. There was nothing really distinctive about the flat; it didn't bear an individual stamp in the way that Peter's house did. After all, the furnishings reflected the tastes of Kevin's mother, not those of Kevin himself. Yet who was to say that mother and son weren't alike? They did seem to enjoy an unusually close relationship.

Kevin interrupted Gabi's thoughts by asking if she enjoyed the music of Johann Strauss. When she nodded affirmatively, he put on a record of Strauss waltzes and asked her to join him in an old-fashioned spin around the well-waxed parquet floor.

"I don't know. . . ." Gabi wasn't sure why she was so hesitant; some ridiculous sense of loyalty to Peter made her unwilling to share physical contact with Kevin.

"Just one dance, a harmless nineteenth-century one at that. Surely one waltz isn't too much to ask."

Gabi gave in, if only to show that she was a good sport. Kevin turned out to be an excellent dancer. When Gabi commented on this, he smiled and murmured something about the advantages of regular practice.

"You must remember that I come from Britain's lower-upper class," he told Gabi. "The only way we can deceive ourselves into thinking that we have anything in common with the upper-upper class is to dress up in white tie and tails or long gowns on every possible occasion and dance to rickety old society orchestras. Naturally, we dance the waltz in lieu of anything you'd see at a disco. Whereas the *real* upper class wouldn't be caught dead dancing anything so old-fashioned as a waltz; they can afford to have fun without losing their upper-crust reputation."

Soon Kevin was showing Gabi how to waltz like a Viennese or at least like an upper middle class Englishwoman. Gabi couldn't help thinking that Kevin would make an ideal partner at a formal ball, where his pleasant good looks, witty manner, and dancing skills would be worthy of the most demanding young noblewoman or debutante. She suspected that his debonair manner was more suited to the London social scene than it was to Switzerland's.

"Enjoying yourself?" he asked when the phonograph had reached the end of the record and shut itself off.

Gabi nodded. "Very much."

"It was kind of you to let me put my arms around you. I was far too shy to do it without having the music as an excuse," Kevin said in a lie so blatant that it made both of them laugh. Suddenly his expression turned serious and he bent his head low to kiss her. Gabi tried to pull from Kevin's gentle but insistent embrace.

"Really, now," he said with good-natured tolerance. "Don't tell me you've never been kissed."

Gabi turned pink at this remark, prompting another observation by Kevin: "I'm sure you've been kissed by that Don Juan employer of yours—that is, when he hasn't been messing about with his ravishing cousin." When Gabi didn't reply, he added: "Don't you think it's time your cheating Lothario got a little of his own back?"

Gabi wasn't sure whom Peter had been cheating: her or Ilse. She supposed Ilse had as much a right to him as she did. Still, a voice inside told her to go ahead and have a little fun of her own. What did she owe Peter, after all?

She tilted her face toward Kevin's and closed her eyes. Her lips were pursed rather than parted, but this didn't discourage Kevin from kissing her with a passion that shocked her with its intensity. Gabi almost pulled away, but she forced herself to accept the kiss when a picture of Peter making love to Ilse flashed across her mind. She did put up a restraining hand when Kevin reached for the buttons on her dress; fortunately, he honored her wishes as Peter never would have done.

When she finally broke free, Kevin's cheeks were flushed, and he was breathing in a way that made Gabi

133

embarrassed. Any pleasure in the kiss had been Kevin's and not hers. She felt cheapened; she had forced herself to go against her own emotions, and this seemed more immoral to Gabi than did the far more passionate lovemaking she had engaged in with Peter. For the first time in her life, she realized that morality involved not only what one did, but why one did it.

Kevin reluctantly dropped his hands from Gabi's arms and looked at her almost sheepishly. "So much for the myth of English reticence," he said with an awkward little laugh.

Gabi managed a wan smile. "It's late, Kevin. I think you'd better take me home."

Kevin maintained a constant stream of patter on the drive to the chalet. Gabi felt sorrier for him than she did for herself; it was obvious that he realized how unimpressed she was by his advances. It wasn't Kevin's fault that his touch brought her no pleasure. Gabi now understood that she was the victim of a fixation that had been taking shape ever since that first interview in Chicago's Drake Hotel.

"Don't bother getting out," Gabi said as gently as she could when they reached the chalet. "I'm sure you'd just as soon avoid Peter if he comes out to see who's here." She hastily stepped out of the little sports car and closed the door behind her.

Kevin rolled down his window to say good-night. "I imagine your real purpose in leaving me here is to avoid the traditional kiss at the front door," he said without resentment.

"Don't be silly!" Gabi said in a burst of affection for this young man who was perfectly likable, even if he didn't inspire love or passion. She bent down and kissed him lightly on the mouth, smiling afterward to hide her mixed reaction to the pressure of his lips against her own. Her gesture of friendship seemed to cheer him up; he grinned happily and threw her a mock salute before heading off toward the main road.

Peter was coming down the staircase when Gabi entered the foyer. She greeted him nervously. Had he seen anything from the upstairs window? When she tried to edge past him so she could go to her room, he grabbed her by the arm. "Come into the living room, will you?" he said, leaving her little choice.

Gabi didn't bother to argue with him. She merely jerked loose from his grasp and continued stubbornly up the stairs. Peter caught up with her just as she reached her bedroom door. Ignoring her muffled protest, he ushered her unceremoniously into the room before following her inside and shutting the door behind him.

"And just what the devil do you think you've been doing?" he asked in an icy tone.

Gabi was too annoyed to give him a response. She turned away from Peter and stared at the French doors leading to the balcony, wondering if her refusal to explain herself would provoke Peter still further.

Peter went on coldly: "I suppose you've been making love with that fainthearted refugee from the West End?"

Gabi's annoyance was replaced by anger at this illogical show of possessiveness. "It's none of your business what Kevin and I have been doing." She added, "How dare you criticize me!"

"How?" Peter moved closer to her, casting a threatening shadow as he stood between Gabi and the light. "You forget that I'm your employer and that you're living in my house. Your behavior with Kevin Fox is a reflection on me."

Gabi couldn't believe her ears. He was talking like a banker or a civil service official, not like an author who wrote witty novels about sexual relationships and professed to believe in individual freedom!

"Well?" he asked, gripping Gabi's left arm. "What do you have to say for yourself?"

"A little over a month ago you were making fun of my innocence, and now you're implying that I'm a . . . a fallen woman."

Peter's mouth twisted in a dangerous-looking smile. "At least I don't have to worry about your losing your virtue at that fellow's hands. Or do I? Perhaps you know how to wrap men like that around your little finger."

"You have no business talking that way about me. Or about Kevin," Gabi said heatedly.

"Come, now. Next you'll be telling me that you aren't like all the other American girls who forget their Puritan heritage once they reach the Continent."

Gabi was tempted to slap him, but she thought better of it when she saw the expression in his eyes. She turned her back on Peter and went to hang her coat in the wardrobe. Before she could take down a hanger, Peter had his hands on her shoulders and was jerking her around to face him.

"There's one way to be sure you won't lose your innocence to our young Mr. Fox, assuming that you haven't done so already," Peter said while reaching for the fastening of Gabi's dress.

"How?" Gabi spat back at him. If only I weren't so vulnerable to his touch, she thought as she tried to ignore the fire that had already begun to course through her veins.

"Very simple. I'll make certain that you lose it to me first." Before Gabi could reply, Peter's lips claimed hers in a searing kiss. The heat of his fingers on her arms, the urgent pressure of his male body against her vulnerable femininity destroyed whatever resistance Gabi had left.

Peter was slowly moving Gabi toward the bed now, using his knees to force her legs into a backward shuffle. His kiss seemed to draw her very soul away; in its place was an emptiness that could be filled in only one way: by an infusion of strength and physical love from Peter.

Physical love. What a meaningless phrase! How could anyone use the word "love" to describe what existed between them, Gabi thought fleetingly before Peter's hands moved inside her dress to brush the filmy bra from the trembling flesh beneath. His palms imprinted their heat on her breasts, the tips of which now sprang to hard points in response to his touch. Love? It's nothing but sexual slavery. But it was too late to resent his power over her, too late to harbor fear or doubts. Gabi felt Peter's right hand graze her buttocks through the dress; she sighed and opened her mouth to him in an unwitting gesture of desire and generosity.

Gabi was lying across the bed now. Peter was taking off her shoes. She couldn't help feeling pleasure in the way his eyes were riveted on her naked breasts.

Oh, Peter! Gabi reached out helplessly with both arms, willing him to come nearer. And then, suddenly, he was uttering a muffled curse and flinging her shoe across the room. "Put some clothes on," he commanded, turning his back on her abruptly and moving toward the bedroom door.

Gabi was stunned. She sat up and hastily pulled the front of her dress across her chest, not bothering to fasten her bra. "I—" She didn't know what to say. Did Peter expect her to apologize for being unable to resist his expert lovemaking?

Peter turned his head around just long enough for Gabi to note that his previously hungry expression had been replaced by one of self-imposed torment. "Why," he asked in exasperation, "did I ever have to become involved with a girl who doesn't know how to look after herself?"

Gabi didn't answer. She was grateful that he was unable to see her own look of anguish as he walked stiffly from the room.

8

~~~~~~~~~

Gabi woke up at six A.M. after spending a restless night in bed. Uncomfortable memories of the previous evening flooded her consciousness before she could get back to sleep, so she forced herself to crawl out of bed and take a shower. She had been meaning to rearrange some of Peter's files; eating breakfast early and starting right in on the filing would at least help to take her mind off Peter's ambivalent attitude toward her.

Frau Maurer was drinking a cup of *milchkaffee* when Gabi entered the kitchen. The housekeeper looked at Gabi with an odd expression but didn't comment on the fact that Gabi was up much earlier than usual. Instead, Frau Maurer brewed more coffee, steamed a pot of milk for Gabi, and apologized for having to serve yesterday's bread since the fresh rolls were still in the oven.

Gabi breakfasted quickly and went upstairs to the library, after brushing her teeth and applying a small quantity of makeup to disguise the shadows under her eyes. She started in on the files but had difficulty concentrating. It was impossible not to think about Peter and his treatment of her the night before.

"I'll make certain you lose your innocence to me first," he had threatened before taking her into his arms. Yet in the end Peter had done nothing of the kind; he had brought her to the peak of arousal and left her. Gabi felt a pang of nausea when she recalled his most humiliating words of all: "Why did I ever have to become involved with a girl who doesn't know how to look after herself?"

To Peter's credit, he hadn't tried to blame her entirely for the incident. His tormented remark had implied that he knew she was the passive, if eager, partner while he was the aggressor. But what solace was there in the fact that Peter regarded her as being hardly more than a child? Surely he wasn't that patronizing with Ilse.

Gabi told herself she should be grateful that Peter hadn't followed through on his intentions. Her conscience may have been overwhelmed by her sensual responses, but if she had given herself to Peter she probably would be regretting it this morning—especially since it was obvious that whatever involvement Peter felt was physical rather than emotional. He had made his feelings clear in their discussion about romantic love, when he'd said that love was seldom anything more than a delusion. His statement that a life of mere compatibility "had its merits" and that he wasn't bothered by Ilse's mercenary attitude certainly hadn't been intended to give Gabi any romantic ideas.

Gabi sighed. Life had become so complicated in the last month or two! If she had met someone like Kevin Fox without having known Peter, would her attitude toward men have been different? Would she have taken Kevin's flattering comments at face value, and would she have been tempted by his wryly delivered suggestion that she become his fiancée?

Kevin wasn't necessarily a bad candidate for marriage. Gabi wondered whether he would formalize his "proposal" if she showed signs of wanting him to do so. Though he appeared to be more firmly tied to his mother's apron strings than most men of his age were, the passion he had shown in kissing Gabi had indicated that he would be more than happy to claim his marital rights once the opportunity arose. Still, Gabi felt distaste at the very thought of sharing a bed with Kevin. There was no question of her even considering a marriage to someone she merely liked, now that she knew what physical passion between a man and a woman could be.

If only there were love between Peter and herself, too! Alas, "love" wasn't the word to use for whatever relationship she and Peter shared, Gabi thought unhappily as she slid papers into manila folders. Peter reacted to her in a way that was almost entirely physical, and as for what she felt toward him . . . it can't be love, Gabi decided with less than full conviction. If it were love, I wouldn't feel so unhappy and confused, she thought. And I wouldn't be as snappish with Peter as he is with me.

Footsteps on the stairs told her that Peter was on his way to the office. Gabi looked at her watch; it was almost nine o'clock. The time had passed more quickly than she had anticipated. She lowered her eyes when the door opened and Peter strode into the room. He stopped half-a-dozen feet from her desk and turned to face her. Slowly, Gabi raised her eyes from the level of his shoes and met his penetrating gaze. What she saw shocked her. Peter's eyes were bloodshot; he had a rumpled appearance even though he was clean-shaven, and his hair was still damp from the shower. He looked exhausted. If he was still angry with her for what had happened the night before, his feelings were very well hidden.

"Good morning." His voice was husky and a little thicker than usual.

"Good morning." Gabi was blushing; she couldn't help herself.

"I hope you're feeling all right after last night?" he asked in a tone that might have been sarcastic but could have been meant to convey no emotion at all.

Gabi inhaled sharply. Usually Peter seemed eager to avoid morning-after confrontations that could interfere with their dictation. Why should today be any different?

"I'll admit I was harsh with you," Peter went on as he moved toward the antique table that served as his desk. He found his chair, sank onto its yielding cushions, and started to fiddle with a penknife and pencil. Gabi watched with fascination while he began to carve a thin strip of wood from the end of the pencil as though he were peeling an apple. He seemed bent on paring away the wood in a single, spiral curl. But his fingers were less sure of themselves than usual, and Gabi couldn't help worrying that the knife might slip.

"You'd better be careful—"

"*Both* of us had better be careful," Peter interrupted, his voice mildly sardonic this time. "I find you dangerously attractive—and you clearly aren't experienced enough with men of my ruthless nature to defend yourself against the primitive instincts you arouse in me and vice versa."

Gabi colored but hastened to his defense. "You aren't ruthless at all," she said, even though she had doubts about her denial. "If you really were ruthless . . ."

"Yes?"

". . . Well, you wouldn't have left me last night," Gabi went on with embarrassment.

Peter managed a cynical smile. "Oh, I would have left you, all right. Only perhaps not at the exact moment I did. You weren't quite ready to send me away, as I recall." He looked down at the pencil, rotated it in his fingers, and carried on with his whittling. "So you see, I am ruthless—only not in the way you thought I meant a moment ago. My 'ruthlessness' could be another word for 'calculation.' No doubt you've been telling yourself for some time that my interest in you as a woman is exceeded only by my desire to avoid frightening off a secretary who might prove difficult to replace."

Gabi didn't answer. She was too hurt by his bluntness to do anything but dig her fingernails into her palms and concentrate on keeping her facial muscles under control.

Suddenly Peter uttered a sharp curse in German and let the pencil and knife clatter to the floor. Gabi looked up to see him squeezing his left forefinger. Blood was pouring from a deep cut, and Peter was trying to keep it from staining the tabletop or his clothing.

"Quick! A handkerchief or tissue if you've got one."

Gabi didn't wait to be told twice. She plunged a hand into her desk drawer, grabbed at a box of tissues, and ran to the antique table. Peter reached to take the box from her, but she was on her knees beside him in an instant, neatly forming a thick pad from the tissues and pressing it around the slashed fingertip.

"I'll run downstairs and have Frau Maurer call for a doctor," Gabi told Peter, her heart pounding from his nearness and from the pain that she shared with him after seeing the cut.

"I don't need a doctor. Frau Maurer is perfectly capable of bandaging me with the help of her first-aid kit."

"But you could get an infection!" Gabi protested. "If germs got into it—"

"No germ would dare infect me," Peter answered with a short laugh. He removed his finger from Gabi's grasp and wrapped another layer of tissue around the cut. His manner was perceptibly cooler now, and he suggested that Gabi should look for Frau Maurer. Sensing his withdrawal, Gabi said nothing further; she reluctantly turned her back on him and went to find the house-keeper.

They began work later than usual because of the time it took to bandage the cut, but Peter still managed to wear Gabi out by dictating nearly fifteen pages before noon. They broke for a leisurely lunch and went back upstairs so that Peter could dictate another short scene. Gabi was more tired than usual but in a warm, happy mood by the time she had transcribed the material and flopped on her bed for a short rest before dinner. She and Peter seemed to get along best when they worked together. It was too bad that their unstrained and friendly office relationship didn't extend to their behavior with one another outside of working hours.

Supper that evening was different from anything Frau Maurer had served on other occasions. It consisted of a large tart filled with sliced apples and garnished with a mound of cottage cheese. Instead of wine, Frau Maurer gave Peter and Gabi large mugs of café au lait.

"Are we economizing?" Gabi asked Peter jokingly when the housekeeper had returned to the kitchen.

Peter shook his head. "Not exactly. You'll recall that we had a heavier lunch than usual."

"I know," said Gabi, thinking of the trout they had eaten at noon. "It left me so full that I was longing for a siesta."

"Tonight's meal is what the rural German Swiss call a 'sweet supper.' It can have a tart, pancakes, porridge, or even rice pudding as the main dish. No doubt it had its origins in the poverty of another era, but I thought you might enjoy seeing how many Swiss country folk still dine today."

Gabi took a bite of the tart and savored it. "What did you eat for suppers as a child?" she asked Peter a moment later.

"We were a fairly prosperous family, and in any case my parents had lived in Zurich for a while after their marriage. Their tastes were on a more sophisticated level than the average Bernese farmer's of that day. Still, we always had our main meal at noon and usually had a simple salad, plate of hash, or sausages for supper." Peter smiled with nostalgia. "Of course, we also ate our share of chocolate, as every Swiss family does. We Swiss have a knack for eating vegetarian dishes and health foods like *birchermuesli* cereal on the one hand and large bars of high-calorie milk chocolate on the other. I'm convinced that every Swiss mother rationalizes those chocolate bars by telling herself that her children are getting an extra portion of milk protein and calcium every time they eat an ounce or two of chocolate."

After dinner, Peter put a hand in the small of Gabi's back and guided her into the living room. Gabi tried to conceal the pleasure she felt from the mere touch of

Peter's fingers through two layers of wool. She longed to be held by him, to snuggle against his chest and feel his warm breath on her hair. Warmth. That was what she needed from Peter: the warm feeling of knowing he cared about her on more than just a sensual level.

"I hope you won't be offended when I say it's high time you learned something about Swiss cooking," he said, settling himself in a chair and picking up a magazine.

"It depends on why you're saying it," Gabi replied, mystified by his comment and wondering if he planned to have her assume the housekeeping duties while Frau Maurer took a vacation.

"I merely thought you might enjoy digging into the roots of your culinary past," Peter said without looking up from the magazine. "You seem to be interested in your Swiss heritage. Cooking is as much a part of that as are history, politics, language, and art."

Gabi couldn't fault his logic. "You're right. I'm sure I'd enjoy learning more."

"Good." Peter's manner now became almost abrupt. "I've already taken the liberty of speaking to Frau Maurer. She's agreed to let you help out with tomorrow night's meal."

Gabi was scandalized by his presumption. How dare he make arrangements for cooking lessons without consulting me first, she thought. He could have asked if she would be interested in helping Frau Maurer with dinner; instead, he was announcing it as a *fait accompli*. "I'm not sure if I want to help Frau Maurer with the cooking," Gabi said stubbornly. "You told me back in Chicago that I wouldn't be expected to prepare your meals."

"Very well, then. Frau Maurer will cook my meal, and

you'll prepare your own. Does that sound fair enough?"
Peter asked with a sudden grin.

Gabi's fury over this example of Peter's treachery
showed in the brilliant green sparkle of her eyes. "You
have a lot of nerve," she told him bitterly.

"I know." Peter's words were uttered deadpan, but his
bland expression quickly gave way to a smile. He took
Gabi's hands in his own and gave them an affectionate
squeeze. "All right. I'll confess that I didn't go about this
the way I should have. Let's try again: Would you like to
join Frau Maurer in the kitchen tomorrow evening and
enjoy a few complimentary lessons on Swiss cuisine?"

Gabi's stubbornness faded. "Since you put it that way,
I'd love to."

"Good. I've suggested that she break you in on *Berner
ratsherrntopf.*"

"My mother used to make that when I was a child,"
Gabi said with delight. "I've always wished that I had her
recipe."

"No doubt Frau Maurer's recipe is comparable." Peter
let go of Gabi's hands and returned to the magazine.

Gabi didn't answer. She looked forward to Frau
Maurer's cooking lesson. Still, she couldn't help feeling a
little disappointed in herself for having given in. Would
she always let herself be swayed from her convictions
when Peter smiled at her and took her fingers in his own?

The next several days were fairly calm for Gabi. Peter
was going out of his way to avoid doing anything that
might compromise their employer-secretary relationship,
though his restlessness showed that the effort was requir-
ing a good deal of self-discipline. He spent one evening

dining and playing cards with Ilse. Gabi had the distinct impression that he was trying to show, through his actions, that he regarded his previous sexual advances as being little more than temporary displays of weakness, which he would take great pains not to repeat in the future. She felt sure that he was again thinking of the bother involved in looking for a new secretary when he was halfway through his book.

Gabi began to learn a variety of recipes from Frau Maurer. The hardest part of Swiss cooking was measuring ingredients by weight rather than volume, she decided after her first attempt at baking. It was strange to weigh out a hundred grams of butter or three hundred grams of flour after years of using teaspoons, tablespoons, and measuring cups. About the only ingredients that were measured by volume were liquids, and even those were doled out in unfamiliar liters or *decis*, the latter containing a hundred milliliters each.

It wasn't long until Gabi could make *schenkeli* or "little thighs," small Bernese fried cookies that resembled their namesake in shape if not in coloring. She became an expert at *äpfelomeletten*, or apple pancakes, and tried her hand at *chriesitütschli*, which were bunches of cherries dipped in a cinnamon-flavored batter and fried in deep fat. Frau Maurer also let Gabi try her hand at several main course dishes and introduced her to a host of Swiss cheeses. Gabi already knew that Swiss cheeses came in varieties other than the familiar Emmentaler with its nutty flavor and many holes. She was nevertheless taken aback by her first taste of *Räss* cheese from Appenzell, which was gray in color and had an extremely pungent flavor.

Gabi assumed that Peter kept track of her progress by

chatting with Frau Maurer on the sly. One day at lunch he tasted a *schenkeli* and complimented Gabi on her baking. She looked down at her plate, unable to suppress a flicker of pride. "I just followed the recipe," she said with unnecessary modesty.

"No doubt you did, but Frau Maurer seems to think you have a natural flair for our Swiss cuisine."

"Don't forget, I was born in Bern," Gabi pointed out.

Peter nodded. "I haven't forgotten. And I also remember promising to take you there soon."

Gabi looked at him hopefully, anticipating that he was going to set a time for the promised excursion. To her disappointment, he returned his attention to the cookies and popped one of them into his mouth before taking another sip of coffee.

Peter was gone during the afternoon while Gabi typed up his latest round of dictation. The book was taking shape nicely, and Peter had begun to ask Gabi for her opinions on any scenes or minor plot complications that he felt needed polishing. He seemed to genuinely value her editorial advice. "Have you ever thought of becoming an editor for a book or magazine publisher?" he had asked one morning after they had discussed one particular scene.

Gabi had shaken her head. "I really don't have any training in that field. Don't forget, I didn't finish college."

"Perhaps not, but you appear well-read and you have a great deal of common sense." He looked at her carefully. "Just what are your long-term goals?"

Peter's question had left Gabi embarrassed. How could she tell him that she had never given much thought to the distant future, since she had always been too busy worrying about making a living in the immediate weeks and months ahead? When her parents were killed, any chance for long-range career plans had been swept away by more immediate problems.

"Very well, I won't press you," he said almost tersely. "No doubt your real interest is in having a husband and family."

"Perhaps," said Gabi, remembering that they had discussed the subject before. "That doesn't mean I wouldn't consider working, though. I might marry a man with his own business. It's too bad there aren't more opportunities for husbands and wives to work together nowadays, the way farmers and owners of small shops manage to do."

"Not to mention writers and editors." Peter had cast a thoughtful look in her direction. "Maybe you'd consider that a practical combination—unless you've come to the conclusion that the two would argue all the time."

Gabi had turned away uncomfortably. Was he making fun of her? "I hadn't even thought about it. I'm a secretary, not an editor."

"So you are." Her words must have irritated Peter in some way, because he had returned to his dictation and hadn't brought up the subject of marriage between writers and their editors again.

Now, as she finished typing Peter's newest section of manuscript, Gabi wondered why he had mentioned the idea at all. Ilse wasn't an editor, was she? He probably thinks I have ambitions in that direction and that I'm convinced I'd make the perfect mate for him, Gabi told herself before yanking the final page from the typewriter. By forcing her to deny those aspirations, he had in effect made her disavow any fantasies of replacing Ilse as his prospective bride. How clever he was, and how much arrogance he showed in thinking she might feel anything but a short-lived physical infatuation toward him!

Gabi brooded over the conversation until dinner, a meal which was centered around meat fritters called *fleischkräpfli* that she had prepared herself under Frau Maurer's supervision. She accepted Peter's compliments politely but without pleasure. When the meal was over, she felt no joy in joining Peter in the living room for their usual coffee by the hearth.

The telephone rang when Gabi was halfway through her demitasse of espresso. She didn't pay any attention to the phone since no one ever called her at the chalet. When Frau Maurer emerged from the kitchen to say that the call was for her, Gabi was taken by surprise.

The caller turned out to be Kevin Fox. "There's a dance at the casino on Saturday; I'd like to invite you to join me. We can have dinner in the casino's dining room before the ball begins."

"Did you say the 'ball'?"

"Oh, yes. It's rather formal—black tie for men, and whatever sort of gown women wear at such functions. You will come, won't you?"

Gabi hesitated. Before she could reply Kevin seemed to make her mind up for her. "I'll pick you up at six-thirty, which will give us time to dine before the dancing begins at eight."

"But I don't have a dress!"

"Then buy one," Kevin said firmly. "You're paid a salary, aren't you? Take some of your earnings and buy a gown. You can't let yourself be locked away in that chalet forever."

Gabi accepted the invitation with mild misgivings. She liked Kevin well enough but wasn't eager to go out with him after what had occurred in his flat. Still, she believed she could trust him not to force his attentions on her if she gave him an unequivocal no.

When Gabi returned to the living room, it was to find Peter looking up from his newspaper and studying her with narrowed eyes. "Who was that?" he asked with a sharpness that Gabi couldn't help resenting.

"Kevin Fox. He's invited me to a ball on Saturday."

Peter's expression turned cooler. "Surely you didn't accept?"

"Of course I accepted," Gabi said, unconsciously drawing herself up to her full height.

"Do you have any idea what his intentions are?" Peter asked dryly.

Gabi refused to be baited. "Not really, but I think I can handle Kevin easily enough," she said rather airily.

"Just as you've handled me?" Peter's lips twisted in a sardonic smile that made Gabi's cheeks glow in humiliation and anger. Having delivered that devastating exit line, Peter set down his coffee cup and went upstairs to edit his manuscript.

When Saturday evening came, Gabi was in a state of nervousness comparable to that which she had felt upon arriving in Thun. She hadn't attended a formal dance in a long time, and she had little idea of what to expect. Gabi had seen only one casino in her life—the one in Monte Carlo—and that had been in a movie. The Monte Carlo casino had looked terribly expensive and sophisticated, being frequented by European millionaires and women of vague continental extraction who wore black velvet evening gowns with mountains of glittering diamonds. Gabi's only valuable pieces of jewelry were her golden Bernese bear on a chain and the tiny diamond earrings, no more than an eighth of a carat each, which she had inherited from her mother. The diamonds of the earrings were set inside little Alpine wildflowers of twenty-three-karat gold. Gabi was reluctant to wear the earrings because she was afraid of losing them, but in the end she decided that she might as well put them on since she had already invested in an equally fancy dress of flame orange georgette. If I'm going to try and look soignée, she thought, I might as well do it right.

She finished adjusting the halter straps of her backless evening gown. The dress was more revealing than Gabi was accustomed to, but the shop clerk had insisted that it was perfect for a ball at the casino. Gabi had finally agreed with the chic saleswoman, in spite of her reservations about baring so much of her creamy skin.

Gabi came downstairs, stepping lightly in her new ballet slippers. She was surprised but relieved to find that Peter wasn't in the living room; no doubt he would have made some scathing remark about her dress had he seen it. Gabi decided that Peter must be keeping out of the way on purpose. She had the feeling that he was being careful to watch his step with her. Perhaps he was feeling the strain of having his desires frustrated so often.

Kevin arrived five minutes late and greeted Frau Maurer politely before helping Gabi into her loden coat. Gabi would have liked to wear an evening cape but hadn't wanted to spend money on a new outer garment after investing nearly a month's salary on her simple but elegant gown. She wanted to save as much out of her earnings as possible so she would have something to live on when her six months with Peter were up.

"That's a lovely dress," Kevin said, admiring the plunging neckline of Gabi's close-fitting bodice. His eyes trailed over the skirt, which flared out until it stopped just above Gabi's toes.

"Thank you." She didn't know why Kevin's gaze made her uncomfortable; his look suggested aesthetic pleasure more than lust. He didn't even touch her bare back when he helped her on with her coat. Perhaps he was recalling Gabi's unresponsiveness during her visit to his flat.

The dining room of the casino was crowded when they arrived, but Kevin had made reservations so there wouldn't be any need to wait in the bar. They were shown to a table for two in the center of the room, where Gabi sensed that she was on display. She tried not to blush when Kevin drew her attention to the many admiring glances that were aimed her way. Self-conscious or not, Gabi couldn't help feeling a certain pleasure in receiving so much attention from total strangers.

"Having a good time?" Kevin asked when they had finished their soup and were beginning the main course.

"Yes, I really am." Gabi savored the delicately poached fish in wine sauce. The champagne that Kevin had ordered went nicely with the fish and left a pleasant tingle on Gabi's tongue each time she sipped it.

"I'd love to show you off to my friends in London," said Kevin. "And, of course, to Mother. You look so dainty tonight—especially in those ballet slippers. Why aren't you wearing heels, by the way? I thought petite women liked to make themselves look taller."

"Oh, I didn't even think about that. I figured it would be easier to dance in ballet slippers than in heels. I feel awkward enough in a long dress as it is. I may be able to avoid tripping on my hem tonight if I'm lucky, but I'd never be able to concentrate on my hemline *and* a pair of spiky heels."

Kevin laughed. "You have no business feeling awkward. You're the belle of the ball. Or you will be, once the music starts in another half-hour or so."

Gabi smiled at his blatant flattery. It was always easier to accept Kevin's compliments than any she got from Peter, since Kevin's were uttered casually and without ulterior motives. If Peter had told her she looked beautiful, it would have meant that he had examined her at length with that probing gaze of his. There was a big difference between being glanced at admiringly and being mentally stripped by a man who appeared to be all too knowledgeable about women and their bodies.

The orchestra had already begun playing when Gabi walked into the ballroom on Kevin's arm. The room was filled with men and women in a variety of clothing styles; some were decked out in full evening regalia, while others wore dark business suits or conservative cocktail dresses. Gabi saw one man, obviously a foreigner, with a broad red sash across his chest and a medal on a purple neck ribbon. She wondered if he could be an exiled king or prince. Switzerland was traditionally a land of political asylum, and Gabi knew that a number of royal pretenders lived within its borders.

Kevin maneuvered Gabi to the dance floor and took

her into his arms with a flourish. They danced to the strains of a Viennese waltz. Gabi's natural grace banished any feelings of self-consciousness once she and Kevin had completed their first swing around the floor.

Tonight Kevin seemed to concentrate on being a charming dance partner rather than a prospective lover or fiancé. Gabi was relieved by this, and she was pleased that he held her at a discreet distance even when the waltz was over and a slower, more intimate, number began. She had no desire to be crushed against Kevin, especially when she was wearing a dress that required her to go without a bra.

Gabi was looking off into the distance, admiring the emerald satin gown worn by a stunning redhead, when she heard a familiar male voice and felt Kevin's arms let go of her body. She jerked her head around and found herself looking into the piercing eyes of her employer.

"I hope you don't mind my cutting in," he said suavely, as he held her at arm's length and let his gaze ravish her figure.

Gabi reddened but made no comment on his appraising look. She didn't want to give Peter the satisfaction of knowing that his relentless masculinity made her uncomfortable at close quarters.

"That's quite a dress." Coming from Peter, the compliment could be interpreted as a veiled insult.

"Thank you," Gabi said with a deeper blush.

"Surely you didn't let your English lover buy it for you?"

"He isn't my lover. Just because you treat women like sex objects doesn't mean every man does," Gabi said. "Anyway, Kevin didn't buy the dress for me. I picked it out myself."

Peter's eyebrows lifted, and his smile became sardonic.

"Actually, the saleslady in the boutique convinced me to buy it," Gabi added hastily. "It did seem awfully . . . well, awfully high-fashion, but she insisted it was the sort of thing I should wear to the ball."

"You do look marvelous in it," Peter conceded. *"Wunderschön,* in fact. There's nothing wrong in wearing so revealing a gown if you don't mind being held by men who want to know your body's secrets." His right hand moved lower on Gabi's back to caress the base of her spine.

They danced silently for a while. Gabi was all too aware of the heat of Peter's hand against her naked skin. His fingertips gently traced the dip in her lower back, sending signals to her nervous system that made Gabi want to cry out in her desire for this man who held her so intimately against his lean male body. She could feel Peter's breath against her hair, could smell the pleasant pungency of his after-shave lotion.

"I must say, I'm rather surprised at your daring tonight," Peter murmured finally.

"Oh?" she replied as she struggled in vain to keep her composure.

"Mmm," he murmured. "That gown reveals almost as much of you as I saw in your bedroom on one memorable occasion."

"Not so loud!" Gabi looked around self-consciously and was relieved to see that no one appeared to have heard Peter's comment, even though it would have been simple enough for anyone to eavesdrop on the crowded dance floor.

They danced in silence until Gabi asked if Peter had come to the ball alone. "Hardly," he answered, jerking his head toward the tables. Gabi glanced in the indicated direction and was met by the angry stare of Ilse Delacroix. Kevin was sitting at Ilse's table and was accepting drinks from a waiter. He didn't appear to resent having to sit with Ilse while his date was in Peter's arms, but Ilse looked as though she would willingly commit murder if she thought she could get away with it. Gabi shivered; she couldn't help being intimidated by the unconcealed hatred on Ilse's face.

Finally the dance ended. As Gabi freed herself from Peter's embrace and turned to leave him, he seized her with a possessive grip on her arm. "Where are you going?" he asked coolly.

"Why—to Kevin, of course."

"Forget Kevin. I want this next dance."

Gabi bridled at his aggressive manner. "Not, 'I want this next dance,' but 'May I have this dance, please?' " she told him tartly.

"Of course you may," Peter smiled at her charmingly, and Gabi had to smile back as he drew her into his arms.

The number to which they were now dancing was a popular and very touching wedding song. The soprano who sang it had a clear, trained voice that reminded Gabi of one of her favorite romantic singers. Gabi sensed that her bare skin was breaking out in goose bumps, and her eyes filmed over with moisture as they did every time she heard the song with its implications of bridal gowns and wedding cakes and shared marital joys. She felt her body being drawn closer to Peter's, and the emotions created in her by the song overcame any resistance she might have had to his embrace. Gabi was thankful that the lights were low; she didn't want Peter to notice how sentimental the song made her feel.

"Let's go back to the house and dance together, just the two of us," Peter said quietly when the song was -over.

"I—I can't." Gabi was tempted by the suggestion but unwilling to leave Kevin in the lurch. "It wouldn't be fair to Kevin. Besides, what would Ilse say?"

"Ilse can get by without my company for one night," Peter said wryly.

The apparent cynicism behind Peter's words was like a red flag to Gabi. How could he speak so callously? Did he really think that women existed only for his casual pleasure, to fall into his arms or retreat discreetly into the background whenever he snapped his fingers? Gabi had little sympathy for Ilse, but she couldn't help being offended by Peter's willingness to temporarily aban- don the woman who seemed destined to become his wife.

"Thank you, but I'd just as soon stay with my escort," Gabi said with a calmness that barely hid her conflicting feelings. She was horrified to realize that she wanted to go with Peter, even though she knew Ilse meant more to him than she ever could.

Peter's tenderness gave way to a cold formality. "Very well. Have fun with your London paramour."

"I've told you he isn't my lover!" Gabi snapped back.

"No? Of course not. I don't suppose he's man enough to be your lover, is he? Which may be why you seem to prefer his company to mine." Peter turned on his heel and strode away from Gabi, leaving her alone in the middle of the dance floor. Gabi tried to ignore the curious glances of the people around her as she walked to the table where Kevin was sitting. She noted with a sinking heart that Ilse was already rushing toward the gaming room where Peter had just gone, an expression of triumph adding a lovely glow to her exquisite features.

9

~~~~~~~~~~~~~~~~~~~

Gabi awoke on Sunday morning to discover that the weather had changed for the worse during the night. She opened the shutters and saw that the balcony outside her room was enveloped in a cold, drizzly fog. The grayness of the day only added to Gabi's already depressed mood.

Peter wasn't in evidence when Gabi went into the kitchen for breakfast. "Herr Peter has gone for the day," said Frau Maurer. "He has instructed me to give you luncheon and supper alone."

The housekeeper gave Gabi a look that was both sympathetic and curious, but Gabi wasn't aware of it. She was too distracted by the hidden meaning that she was trying to find in Peter's message. Had Peter meant to imply that she was being punished for not giving in to his invitation at the casino? Was he suggesting or even warning that she shouldn't plan on spending the evening with Kevin Fox in his own absence? Or was the message that she should eat without him free of any implications? Somehow the latter seemed almost too straightforward a possibility; Gabi wanted very badly to fault Peter for devious behavior.

Gabi's appetite was almost nonexistent this morning, but she managed to eat a light breakfast to keep Frau Maurer from suspecting that her evening at the ball hadn't been a total success. The housekeeper might guess the truth about her feelings for Peter if she weren't careful. Gabi didn't think she could live with the embarrassment that would come from such a humiliating disclosure.

"You're not hungry?" Frau Maurer asked with an expression of concern when Gabi rose from the table after eating only one roll.

Gabi shook her head. "It must be the weather," she mumbled. How could she admit that she hungered only for Peter, the man she loved?

The man I love. Those blunt and simple words stunned Gabi as they flashed through her like a bolt of lightning. Until this morning, Gabi hadn't acknowledged the true nature of her feelings toward Peter. She had always tried to convince herself that her desire for Peter was only physical and could be kept in check through rigorous attempts at self-denial. The fact that she hadn't been able to control her behavior in Peter's arms had meant only that she was too naive to deal with a lover of Peter's experience, or so she had told herself until now.

Now she knew the truth. When Peter had walked from the ballroom of the casino with Ilse trotting after him, Gabi had felt a horrible emptiness in her heart. It was as if a part of her soul had been taken away and banished to a limbo from which it would never return.

Gabi fled upstairs to the bathroom before Frau Maurer could notice her gathering tears. I've been so foolish, she thought. The only way to compete with someone like Ilse is to fight on her own terms.

And yet, what were those terms? Did Peter expect her to go to bed with him, to abandon the values she had been raised with so that he could compare her performance to Ilse's and see who was the better woman?

Gabi colored, even though there was no one to see her. It wasn't long before the flush of humiliation gave way to the heat of anger and resentment. She told herself that going to bed with Peter might not benefit her in any case; he and Ilse came from a common background, shared a sophistication that Gabi could never aspire to, and were joined by a common interest in their late uncle's estate. At least, money was one of the reasons Ilse wanted Peter, even if it wasn't a reason for his being interested in her. Or so Kevin had said when describing the erosion of his own romance with Ilse.

If only I'd come back to the chalet with Peter last night! Gabi told herself in defiance of all logic, while splashing cold water on her face in the hope of returning her cheeks to their normal color. She should have returned with him, not to compete with Ilse, but rather to seek the fulfillment that she could find only in Peter's arms. It would be better to experience the joy of his lovemaking at least once in her life, even if she couldn't hope to keep him.

The weather was too miserable to make a walk worthwhile, and there wasn't much point in taking a postal bus into Thun on a Sunday. Gabi dried her face and climbed the stairs to the library. It was a good day for reading; all she had to do was find something interesting and curl up in the leather armchair beneath the glass skylight.

She had already read every magazine that was worth leafing through, so she began combing the bookshelves with a more discriminating eye than usual. Presently she came upon a volume she hadn't seen before: a thin German book titled *Joachim und Gisela* that had Peter's name on the spine. Gabi took the book from the shelf, turned to the copyright page, and saw that the book had been published seven years earlier. A glance at the author's biography on the dust jacket told her that this was Peter's first novel.

Gabi made herself comfortable in her armchair and began reading. It soon became obvious that this book was considerably different from Peter's novel in progress. It had the classic first-novel plot of a young man growing up and falling in love for the first time. And yet, despite the lack of anything unusual in the story line, the book had a brilliance and poignancy that Gabi found breathtaking. The characterizations were extremely sharp, and the writing—in *Hochdeutsch,* or High German—was almost poetic. Gabi made a mental note to read more of Peter's German writings in the future; he was an excellent writer in English but seemed nothing short of a genius in his native tongue.

Gabi became absorbed by the well-drawn portrait of the young man. The hero's girlfriend also came across as an extraordinarily sympathetic young woman. There was something vaguely familiar about this female character; Gabi couldn't place her, but the girl seemed reminiscent of a heroine that she must have run across in some other novel.

Two other things about the book were especially striking to Gabi: the tenderness and depth of feeling in the love scenes, and what the novel showed about the personality of its author. Gabi sensed a fierce independence in the book's main character. *Joachim und Gisela* clearly had been written by a man who refused to be shackled by society's conventions, even though he had a rigorous moral code of his own.

Gabi skipped lunch in order to finish the novel before Peter's return. She put the volume on the shelf a little after four o'clock and went to her room, where she lay on her bed and tried to sort out her confused thoughts. Could the Peter Imhof who had abandoned her on the dance floor last night be the same man who wrote *Joachim und Gisela* seven years ago?

The answer must be no, Gabi told herself even as she longed to be in Peter's arms. The young man in the novel never would have fallen for a woman as transparently mercenary as Ilse seemed to be. Peter must have changed in the years that had elapsed since the writing of his book. Why he had changed was unimportant; what counted was that it was too late to bring the old Peter back.

On that unhappy note, Gabi rose from the bed and went to the bathroom, where—for the second time that day—she splashed cold water on tear-stained cheeks.

Gabi heard a knock at her bedroom door the next morning before she had changed out of her nightgown. She quickly slipped into her bathrobe and opened the door to Peter, who was nattily attired in a dark gray suit of herringbone tweed.

"How would you like to go to Bern?" Peter asked Gabi. Without waiting for her reply he said, "You might want to wear something fairly dressy, since we'll be lunching with a member of the Federal Council."

Gabi was too astonished to respond. The Swiss Federal Council was similar to the Presidential Cabinet in the United States, except that the individual members were elected rather than appointed and took turns being President of the Confederation for a year at a time.

Peter smiled. "I suppose you're wondering why a novelist is having lunch with a member of such an august government body."

"It isn't an everyday occurrence, is it?" Gabi said, as she self-consciously tightened the knot of her robe's terrycloth belt.

"Not really. The Swiss branch of the International P.E.N. Club is drafting a statement on political oppression of dissident writers in other countries, and I've been asked to write the preliminary document. Herr Ringgenberger of the Federal Council has agreed to outline the government's position on the matter."

"But what do you need me for?" Gabi asked awkwardly.

"You're my secretary. You can take minutes of our meeting or simply keep notes in your head, as you prefer." Peter rested a hand on Gabi's shoulder, sending a responsive shiver down her back. "Being a former absentminded professor, I don't dare entrust the honorable councilor's words to my own memory."

As soon as Peter had left her alone, Gabi put on her best taffeta slip and took a softly tailored dress of cobalt-colored knit from her wardrobe. It had black buttons and a self-belt that knotted at the waist. She decided to wear her golden Bernese bear on its 18-karat chain and chose a silk scarf in a bright rainbow pattern, which she had bought in Zurich's Jelmoli department store the day she got off the plane. At the time she hadn't realized how high the scarf's price was when converted into dollars.

Gabi joined Peter for a quick breakfast; soon they were

on their way to Bern. The federal and cantonal capital was less than half an hour away by road. Gabi felt an odd exhilaration as the car neared the city where she and her parents had been born. Though she had been only a year old when she left her native city, she recognized its outstanding features from photographs: the steeple of the *münster* or Protestant cathedral, the red-tiled roofs, the domes of Parliament, the steep tree-covered slopes that led down from the high plateau of the inner city to the River Aare, which made a sharp 180-degree curve to enclose the city's core on three sides. Peter parked the car in a garage on the edge of the old town and led Gabi on foot to the Federal Parliament Building.

Since they had more than an hour until their luncheon appointment, they joined a public tour. Gabi listened to the usher's description of the National Council and the Council of States, which were roughly comparable to the House of Representatives and the Senate in the United States. She learned that the seven-member Federal Council, to which Herr Ringgenberger belonged, was elected by the two legislative bodies and nearly always represented the country's four major political parties, thanks to a tradition that had been in force for many years.

Peter commented on the Swiss system of government during a break in the lecture. "We're such a diverse country, with so many ethnic and political viewpoints, that gentlemen's agreements are used to make sure that every party or national group of any size is represented fairly."

"And the President?" asked Gabi. "How much power does he have?"

"Not a great deal. First of all, he serves for only a

one-year term. He has no more authority than his colleagues on the Federal Council and functions mostly as a chairman at Council meetings. In fact, he continues to run his assigned ministry even while he serves as President."

"Switzerland must not have many problems on a national scale," said Gabi.

"Oh, I don't know. We have difficulties just as other countries do. But there's little need for a powerful central government, since no government would dare make sweeping changes in response to a particular issue. The Swiss people would never stand for that; we're a conservative race by nature."

Later, as she and Peter neared the end of the tour, Gabi remarked on the apparent lack of security in the Parliament Building. There were relatively few guards about, and many of the rooms used by the nation's top officials were left open when they weren't being occupied.

"I suppose it's because we Swiss frown on the heavy trappings of office that are found in many other countries," Peter explained. "Even the President rides the tram to work without a bodyguard. I doubt if he's in much danger; most people wouldn't recognize him if they bumped into him on the streetcar."

Herr Ringgenberger of the Federal Council met Peter and Gabi in the main entrance foyer at twelve o'clock. He had already booked a table in the Kornhauskeller, a former grain and wine storehouse which was now a well-known restaurant. They walked the few blocks to the Kornhauskeller; soon Gabi was being led into a huge room with balconies and a wide staircase overlooking a vast sunken dining area.

"What a marvelous room!" Gabi said, admiring her surroundings while Herr Ringgenberger conferred with a headwaiter.

"Believe it or not, the Kornhauskeller has a 10,000-gallon beer keg that's big enough to wet the whistle of every man in Bern," Peter told her.

It wasn't long until they were seated and then joined Herr Ringgenberger in a discussion of the government's position on literary freedom in other countries. Gabi was kept busy following the rapid flow of German. She even scribbled on a notepad from time to time in case Peter asked her to repeat Herr Ringgenberger's more important remarks later on.

Eventually the business conversation gave way to small talk. Gabi's mind began to wander as she toyed with the rest of her lunch. She looked at Peter's bold, intelligent features and found herself thinking how proud she would be to spend her life at this man's side—to help him with his work, to bear his children, and to share his joys and disappointments. Such fantasies were pointless; Gabi knew that Peter would marry Ilse if he decided to take a wife at all. Just because he's sometimes tempted to go to bed with me doesn't mean he'll ever fall in love with me, Gabi warned herself. She tried to turn her mind to other things before her expression could reveal the tormented feelings inspired by her hopeless love for Peter.

Gabi and Peter didn't leave the restaurant and Herr Ringgenberger until two o'clock. Gabi had assumed that they would go home directly after the meeting, but Peter surprised her by suggesting that they see more of her hometown.

They visited the arcaded streets of the shopping district, where Gabi admired the seventeenth- and eighteenth-century houses and marveled at how many expensive-looking flower shops and candy stores called *confiseries* were to be found in this city of only 165,000 people. She was equally delighted by the uniform appearance of the old city, which seemed to be built almost exclusively of pale sandstone.

With Peter acting as her personal guide, Gabi watched the animated figures go around on the famous medieval clock tower and took pleasure in the many wonderfully carved stone fountains. Later in the afternoon, they saw the bear pits, which had been popular with Bernese and tourists alike since the 1400's. The bear was, of course, the official mascot and heraldic symbol of Bern, a name that Gabi assumed was a corruption of the German word *bären,* or "bears."

It was going on six o'clock when they finished all of the sightseeing that Gabi could manage in her attractive but not very practical dress shoes. "Since it's so late, we might as well have supper in Bern," Peter said to Gabi. "I've already told Frau Maurer not to expect us."

Gabi looked at him uncertainly. "We had an awfully big lunch. I'm really not very hungry."

"In that case, we'll go to one of my favorite eating places in Bern: a little coffee shop high up in the railroad station. It's seldom crowded, since it's in such an out-of-the-way location that most travelers don't even know it exists. You can order as much or as little as you like."

The restaurant did look like an attractive version of a tiny American coffee shop with its U-shaped counter and small tables. Gabi and Peter sat next to a glass wall that overlooked the many railroad tracks leading into the station. They dined on sausages and potato salad while taking turns attempting to identify the nationalities of foreign railway cars that were mixed in with the dark green Swiss trains. Gabi could understand why Peter was so fond of this restaurant, which was homey and friendly in spite of its modern setting. She was delighted when a man came in with his wire-haired fox terrier and the waitress gave him a soup plate filled with scraps for the dog to eat on the floor while the man had his own dinner.

There was a pronounced crispness in the air when Gabi and Peter walked back to the garage near Parliament. Gabi was nevertheless warmed by Peter's arm around her shoulders as they followed a promenade overlooking the River Aare. The path was illuminated by soft streetlamps; the mist of early evening put the buildings and trees in soft focus, making Gabi feel as if she were part of a scene in a romantic film. For the first time in days, Gabi felt at peace with Peter and with herself. She knew she was the victim of a temporary dream, that this feeling of utter contentment wouldn't last, but she relaxed in hopes of enjoying it while she could.

Gabi didn't protest when Peter stopped in a secluded spot near the *münster* and took her into his arms. She felt his hands slip inside her loden coat, felt the potent evidence of his need as he drew her body against his own. "Oh, Peter . . ." she murmured.

"Hush." His lips molded themselves against hers with a possessive ardor that left her breathless and weak-kneed. His mounting desire for her was revealed by the strength of his embrace, by the deep rhythmic probing of his tongue inside her mouth, and by the forcefulness with which he was shaping her softly yielding body against the rigid length of his own. Yet there was a gentler side to his lovemaking, too: a pattern of tender caresses and affectionate squeezes that implied a genuine caring, as though

171

he were trying to establish a degree of spiritual and emotional intimacy. For Gabi, this was rapture, or the closest thing to rapture that she was ever likely to enjoy with this enigmatic yet irresistible man.

Gabi was surrendering to her love and her own growing desire for Peter when he took his hands from her breasts with a resigned sigh. Her eyes flashed open to see him inspecting her carefully. She lowered her gaze in an irrational act of shyness that caused her to miss the revealing expression that briefly crossed Peter's face. When she looked up again, his features betrayed no emotion. "We'd better be on our way before we commit a sacrilege in the very shadow of the cathedral," he whispered. Gabi took Peter's arm and was grateful that he hadn't adopted the remote air that he sometimes displayed after resisting the temptation to make love to her.

Ten minutes later, they were on their way home in the vintage Porsche. Gabi noticed after a while that they were taking an unfamiliar route. When she commented on this, Peter explained that he had thought it would be more pleasant to take a quieter, slower way back. "Of course, if you're in a hurry—"

"Not at all." Gabi was pleased that he was taking the detour for her sake or because he enjoyed her company. The intimacy they had enjoyed by the *münster* hadn't yet been shattered; there was still hope that the evening would end on a tender note.

Peter's voice interrupted her thoughts. "Have you given any thought to what you'll do when your six-month trial period is up?"

Gabi hesitated. I had wanted to go on working for you, she longed to say, but with Ilse in the wings there was no point in giving such an answer. Instead, she gave voice to an idea that kept recurring now that she was almost certain that his future lay with Ilse: "I know I promised to stay a minimum of six months—"

"That's right. A minimum." Peter's eyes moved from the road to her face, and Gabi saw that an inexplicable tension had taken hold of his features. "You aren't thinking of breaking that promise?" he asked seriously. "I thought we'd been over that ground before."

"I won't break it unless I have good reason to." Gabi's tone was light even if her feelings weren't.

"In that case, there's no need for either of us to worry. I don't intend to give you a reason, good or bad, to quit before six months are up." As if to reassure her, Peter reached out and placed a hand on her left thigh. Gabi couldn't help sensing a fiery inner tingling at the weight of his fingers on her leg, although she concealed her feelings from Peter by making an offhand remark about the scenery. In a little while he put his hand back on the gear lever to downshift for a hairpin curve. When they were on the straightaway again, his fingers moved to the steering wheel and his foot pressed on the accelerator.

For the first time, she wondered if the vaguest beginnings of a relationship other than physical now existed between them. Perhaps it wasn't love—not from Peter's viewpoint, anyway—but at least it was an emotional commitment, a bond of affection, that seemed to go beyond an employer's casual interest in his secretary and vice versa. Could Peter be having second thoughts about Ilse? Was it remotely possible that he would turn away from his cousin in the end, ignoring her beauty and cool sophistication in order to nurture the seed of love that he had planted in Gabi's own heart?

I'm being a fool, Gabi warned herself. But then, she had always been a fool where Peter was concerned. She wasn't asking that he return her love immediately; she asked only that Peter not slip a ring on Ilse's finger within the next six months. If he decided at the end of the probationary period that Ilse would make the more suitable wife, Gabi could return to the United States or find a position elsewhere in Switzerland, so she wouldn't have to endure the pain of being around for the wedding. If, on the other hand, he decided after six months that Ilse was far too shrewd and calculating to make an acceptable bride . . . But no; Gabi didn't dare put that hope into words. All she would do was keep her fingers crossed and her jealousy under control until spring.

Gabi's pulse was racing from a growing tension when they reached the chalet. Peter had touched her several more times during the journey, his fingers seeming to stamp her with a symbol of his possession whenever they encountered her willing flesh. What would happen once they were inside the house? Would Peter maintain the self-control that he had shown by the cathedral in Bern, or would it be her responsibility to call a halt to their lovemaking if things got out of hand? How could she possibly say no when Peter's tender caresses and penetrating kisses made her body cry yes?

Peter drove the little coupé into the garage and walked around to open the passenger door for Gabi. His steady hand took hold of her own trembling fingers and drew her gently from the Porsche and into his embrace.

Gabi's loden coat was being opened again; experienced fingers undid the buttons of her dress and moved inside to unhook her bra. Gabi reacted without fear or shyness when Peter cupped her breasts in his hands and bent down to kiss the swelling, hardening nipples. It was cool in the garage, but the flames ignited by Peter's lips were more than enough to warm Gabi. Yes, she murmured silently. She couldn't give Peter money, or power, or prestige, but she could give him love, and she could offer him her innocence. Somehow Gabi trusted that Peter would not accept her gift unless he could return it with at least a partial commitment of his own.

Something warm and furry moved against Gabi's leg. She looked down and saw Winifred, the sheep dog, beaming up at her with soft brown eyes. For a moment she had a sinking feeling, convinced that the interruption would bring Peter to his senses. If he withdrew now . . . Please don't let him! she begged silently, trying to invoke a telepathic power over the man whose face was only now lifting itself with obvious reluctance from the perfumed skin between her breasts.

"Peter—"

He shushed her by touching his fingers to her trembling lips. "Winifred seems to be telling us that we'd be more comfortable in the house," he said as he buttoned Gabi's dress without bothering to hook her bra. He was looking directly into her eyes now, his expression nothing less than a visual challenge—a challenge to abandon all fear and innocence; a challenge to forget about looking back and to accept the inevitable.

They were holding hands when they emerged from the garage. The sky was clear and black, with stars scattered across it like glittering diamonds on black velvet. Gabi looked up and saw constellations she hadn't thought about since her childhood: Ursa Major, the Great Bear, its body encompassing the Big Dipper; Orion, the slain hero of Greek legend, who had been placed in the sky by the huntress Diana to roam the celestial équator until the end of time. Even the stars of the Milky Way seemed to stand out from each other tonight. How small we are, Gabi thought before realizing with utter clarity that tonight the universe for her was centered on one man: Peter.

They reached the door of the chalet. Peter slid the key into the lock. Gabi heard the door swing open and felt Peter lifting her in his arms to carry her across the threshold like a groom with his new bride. He didn't put her down, but instead carried her to the staircase and mounted the steps confidently while his lips trailed kisses along her delicate jawline before coming to rest on her soft lips. The hem of her skirt had fallen back, uncovering her thighs. She felt the whisper of a draft on her exposed legs and thought dreamily of being warmed by Peter's naked body.

Peter took her to his bedroom, which she'd only caught momentary glimpses of before. It was a large, traditionally furnished room with a masculine-looking pine wardrobe and chest of drawers, together with a massive bed that looked as though it had been hewn with axe and adze more than a century earlier. He deposited her upright on the sheepskin rug at one end of the bed. Without a word, he began to unfasten the buttons of her dress. Only the delicate flush of renewed shyness that touched Gabi's cheeks when he stripped away the garment hinted that she wasn't used to being undressed by men in strange bedrooms.

Her bra was still unhooked. Gabi expected Peter to remove it as he had the dress, but he surprised her by stepping back and regarding her with a serious expression. "The next step is up to you," he said quietly.

Was he really offering her a choice? And if so, was he doing it out of consideration or a desire to humiliate her? A dozen conflicting thoughts fought for supremacy inside her head, and it took only seconds for one to emerge as the victor: I need him as much as he needs me. Probably more. With that, Gabi slipped the bra from her shoulders, and let it drop to the floor. She faced Peter squarely, without shyness this time, wanting him to see the erect nipples and flushed skin of her breasts.

Then Gabi kicked off her shoes and reached down to remove her panty hose. She was wearing nothing but the briefest of bikini panties now: a wisp of pale gauze-like nylon that tantalized rather than concealed. She recognized the desire in his gaze and felt a rush of satisfaction. There was something else in his look too—an expression of appreciation, of tenderness, of masculine approval. In asking her to take off her own clothes, he had been making her show that she was a participant in their lovemaking and not merely a passive partner.

Gabi was about to step out of her underpants when Peter leaned forward and took her wrists in his hands. "Not yet." Leading her to the wardrobe, he opened the heavy pine doors and took out a knee-length kimono of blue-and-white silk. He slipped it over her arms and tied it loosely at the waist. Then he led her to the bedside and perched her on the edge of the firm mattress, wrapping her shoulders carefully in a goosedown *decke* before moving to the tile stove in one corner of the room.

While Gabi watched, Peter built a fire in the stove and shut its heavy cast-iron door. He disappeared into the connecting bathroom without a word, returning three or four minutes later in a lightweight robe of navy blue wool. He sat on the bed, lifted the goosedown comforter from Gabi's shoulders, and drew her onto his lap. His fingers undid the knot in the kimono's belt and moved beneath the sensuously clinging fabric to rest on her abdomen. Gabi inhaled sharply when his hand wandered tantalizingly over the soft skin of her stomach. She let her breath out slowly when he lifted his fingers again and moved them to her right breast, where they slowly traced a circle around the rosy proof of her arousal.

When Peter spoke again, his voice was gentle but disconcertingly serious. "Gabi, I think the time has come to discuss our feelings for each other."

"No!" I can't bear that, she thought in a panic, jerking her knees together in an involuntary reaction to what she feared he might tell her. Then, tremblingly, "Some things are better left unsaid."

Peter's expression became quizzical, but he didn't release his hold on her shoulders. "I should have spelled things out a long time ago—"

"Don't." He was trying to be fair; Gabi knew that. He was obviously trying to explain, as diplomatically as he could, that whatever happened tonight wouldn't reduce the likelihood of his marrying Ilse. I don't want to know, Gabi thought with desperation. If I can't live for tomorrow, then for God's sake let me enjoy what's left of today.

She heard Peter sigh. "Very well." There was an accepting quality in his voice, as though he had decided not to concern himself with what she might feel in the morning. He reached across to the nightstand and turned off its small lamp. The room's only illumination now came from the dancing flames behind the mica window in the door of the tile stove.

Any lingering thoughts of the future were shunted

aside almost immediately by the sensuous way in which Peter slid Gabi's kimono off and tossed it to the floor alongside the bed. He could no more turn back than she could, now that the restraint of clothing had been stripped from their bodies.

Suddenly he was alongside her, drawing her into his arms and plundering her mouth with a deep kiss while his hands roved over her hips until he found the dimples on either side of her spine. Gabi arched toward him, straining with the need to assuage her mounting passion.

She felt Peter's lips move to her breasts, the tip of his tongue igniting little brushfires of pleasure even as his knee nudged her legs apart. "Oh, yes!" she heard herself gasp. And then she was opening herself to him, taking him deep into her very being.

A moment's pain surrendered to far more glorious sensations: a warmth that began as a tiny pinpoint of pleasure and spread outward until her whole body was like one vast, throbbing nerve ending. Each sensual movement, each caress of Peter's exploring fingertips taught Gabi things about her body and its responses that she had never known before. She felt Peter roll onto his back, felt herself being lifted up and taken with him, so that she lay with her tingling nipples flattened against the muscular expanse of his chest. His fingers and palms were now stroking her, massaging her, tracing her feminine curves, and spurring her on to establish a rhythmic pace of her own. What could have been an act of domination instead became an act of sharing. Gabi felt tears streaming down her face but didn't care. If she was crying, it was from happiness. What she and Peter were sharing at that moment was something that would live on in her memory forever.

The explosion of joy that came next caught Gabi unawares. Spiraling desire burst into something altogether more powerful: a gasping, ecstatic release that was followed by the tightening of Peter's arms around her body and a deep, shuddering groan. For a moment, Gabi was a star in the center of a contracting universe, one over which she as co-creator had willingly relinquished all control.

Afterward, Gabi opened her mouth to tell Peter that she loved him—but he quieted her with a kiss. He wrapped her in the goosedown comforter and touched his lips briefly against her tangled hair. He murmured to her, offering a gentle endearment. I love you, she wanted to respond. *Ich liebe dich.* But her throat was dry, her mind was already wandering, and her body was exhausted. I love you. The words, not spoken but existing merely in her head, echoed and faded. Gabi was already sinking away from consciousness and into sleep.

When she awoke, it was to find Peter sleeping beside her, his body fully exposed to her shy and curious gaze. The fire in the tile stove had died down; the room was becoming cool. Gabi unwrapped herself from the warm comforter and spread it over Peter, taking care not to wake him. Then she slipped into the borrowed kimono and went into the hall. She had no real plan or destination in mind; she simply had to get away from Peter and think for a little while. She moved slowly in the direction of the staircase and climbed the steps to the library.

The first thing she noticed when she entered the room was the copy of *Joachim und Gisela* that she had read when Peter was out of town. Her eyes were drawn immediately to the colorful dust jacket, and she walked to the shelf as though drawn by a power that she couldn't quite understand. Almost against her will, she took the novel from the wooden shelf and opened it. Her eyes scanned the pages quickly until she found a scene that had moved her deeply when she'd read the book. It was the scene where Joachim first made love to his Zurich-born sweetheart, and where the misunderstandings that had plagued their relationship all along were finally swept away on a tide of shared ecstasy.

Gabi closed her eyes. She thought of all the books she'd read in which a momentous importance was attached to the loss of virginity. Well, she had lost hers. And was her life so very different now? Not really. She had thrilled to his caresses, of course, and she'd rejoiced in the unprecedented intimacy that she had felt as she and Peter had lain naked in each other's arms. But was she any happier? Hardly. Nor was she any less happy, if only because she had already experienced the depths of despair every time she had thought of Peter's eventual rejection of her in favor of Ilse.

Her eyes blurred with tears as she returned her attention to the scene in Peter's novel. Joachim and Gisela had just awakened after dozing off together and were explaining their feelings to each other as a prelude to continued lovemaking. Having given herself fully to Peter, Gabi could understand the joy and confusion that existed side by side in the heroine's mind. She could see, too, just how perceptive Peter had been in his description of the girl's feelings. If only she, like Gisela, could look forward to a happy ending.

She was about to close the book and search for a tissue when the floor creaked behind her. As she turned around, two strong arms encircled her shoulders, and she

181

bumped headlong into Peter, who was dressed in the same robe that he'd worn downstairs. The bathrobe was knotted loosely at the waist, exposing a generous expanse of chest hair. Gabi averted her eyes. There was something altogether too sensual about the proximity of his naked skin. An image of their lovemaking flickered into her mind and was immediately suppressed as she battled for emotional self-control. Once is enough, the voice of common sense warned. She had begun to hope, in retrospect, that making love with Peter just one time would make her immune to future temptation. Yet she wanted him again now—and it was a desire that she had to get rid of at all costs, since she didn't dare become more dependent on him than she already was.

"You're fighting it," he said quietly. "Why?"

Gabi somehow resisted the impulse to throw caution to the winds. "Fighting what?" she asked with unconvincing calmness.

"What you feel for me."

She bit her lip. Her cheeks became hot with self-conscious shame even as she felt a terrible ache somewhere inside her. "I suppose you mean sex," she said bitterly, surrendering what was left of her pride.

"I had hoped the word might be 'love.'"

Gabi stared at him. No, she thought. I can't have heard correctly.

"You've been reading *Joachim und Gisela*," he went on in a gently perceptive voice. "It wasn't just my first novel. It's also the only one of my books to reveal anything of my own youthful dreams and feelings."

Gabi tried to ignore the growing pressure of his fingers on her arms. His voice had taken on an intense quality, even if his tone was gentle, and his eyes were boring into hers in a mercilessly probing way. "Are you trying to tell me that you have someone like Gisela in your past?" she asked with a lightness that she didn't feel.

"Not in my past. In my present. And, if I'm very lucky, in my future."

Gabi's spirits soared for an instant before she firmly suppressed the fantasies that had been dominating her thoughts ever since she'd recognized her love for Peter. No, she warned herself. You can't stand another disappointment.

"If you'd read the whole book—" Peter continued.

"But I have."

His stare became more quizzical. "If that's true, you shouldn't have any trouble understanding my feelings for you. The heroine in *Joachim und Gisela* should remind you of someone you've known for a long time."

When enlightenment truly dawned on Gabi, Peter let go of her arm and touched his fingers to lips that had begun to quiver with pent-up emotion. "Yes. The girl in the book is a lot like you. If I weren't afraid of sounding melodramatic, I'd say you were the kind of woman I've been looking for all my life."

"But Ilse—"

"My clinging cousin, who pursues me so intently for the sake of my money? What about her? I've been all too patient with her as it is; I certainly don't want her intruding on my pleasure when I'm alone with you."

"But I thought—"

He looked at her carefully for a moment, and then a smile slowly spread across his face. "So you *were* jealous. I thought so, at first. But when you kept fighting me at every turn, I began to wonder if you disliked her for some more basic reason. I can hardly blame you for resenting her, even if I didn't enter into your feelings. Ilse can be an awful snob."

Before Gabi could reply to this, Peter was drawing the lapels of her kimono apart and kissing the hollow of her neck with an exquisite, lingering tenderness that sent sparks along the nerves that led to the very center of her responsiveness. She was flowering again, blossoming under his expert touch, only this time she knew that his caress symbolized something beyond the physical: a thing she had never dared hope for, an emotion called love.

"I've always thought of myself as a confirmed bachelor," Peter went on when he had drawn himself erect and pulled her trembling body against his own. "When I first suspected that you meant more to me than the other women I'd known, I was afraid to express my feelings, because I wasn't sure you'd reciprocate. Once it became obvious that you were attracted to me, I had to control myself because I couldn't bear the thought of letting you have your freedom later on if you changed your mind. I could tell from your reactions to my kisses that you'd never been in love before—and I wouldn't have been able to forgive myself if I'd taken you to bed without being sure that you weren't just going through a temporary infatuation."

"And your . . . other women?" It wasn't the most diplomatic of questions, but it was one that Gabi had to ask.

"There have been a few. I'm a man, not a boy."

"Women like Mary Cleaver, your secretary in Vermont?"

Peter looked at her in surprise. "Mary Cleaver? She was never anything but my secretary. Besides, she was happily married to another man." His eyes widened. "Surely you didn't think—"

"I didn't know what to think," Gabi murmured, coloring with shame.

Peter's lips bent in a self-deprecating smile. "You really thought the worst of me, didn't you? I suppose I deserved it after the way I behaved in order to hide my true feelings for you. But now we both know the truth. I know I can't live without you and—"

"You know that I can't live without *you*," Gabi broke in.

He nodded gently. "Yes, I can tell from our lovemaking that you need me as much as I need you."

Our lovemaking. What a perfect phrase, Gabi thought dreamily as she surrendered to the joy of being closer to Peter than she'd ever felt before. His hands were on her breasts now, and his robe had opened to reveal the bold evidence of his rising need for her. She heard him murmur something about the Swiss custom of hyphenated married names. "Frau Gabriele Studer-Imhof," he was saying. "It has a nice sound. I should have made you try it on for size earlier."

A quiet chuckle escaped Peter's throat, and Gabi's kimono somehow slipped to the floor. The navy blue robe and their two bodies followed. Arms and legs opened in welcome; flesh became lost in flesh, and two lovers were united in a clinging embrace. *"Ich liebe dich,"* Gabi whispered, her mind reverting for the moment to the speech of her childhood. A tide of heady sensations robbed her of all capacity for further speech, making her demonstrate her feelings in more intimate ways instead. As she clung to Peter, as she quivered with joy beneath this man who was soon to become her husband, her eyes opened for a second to glance involuntarily at the window and see the lake, the mountains, and the first rays of the rising sun. It was as though Gabi had just discovered a new world. *Their* world. A world that would be waiting for the two of them when the intensity of the moment had given way to a shared tenderness, and they could stand together at the window overlooking Lake Thun, their arms around one another, to kiss once again as they greeted the new dawn.